120 rue de la Gar

Léo Malet was born in _____ _al education and began as _____ 'e' in Montmartre in 1925 _____ uted to various magazines: *L'Insurge, journal de ___ Sandales* . . . He had various jobs: office worker, ghost writer, manager of a fashion magazine, cinema extra, newspaper seller . . .

From 1930 to 1940 he belonged to the Surrealist Group and was a close friend of André Breton, René Magritte and Yves Tanguy. During that time he published several collections of poetry.

In 1943, inspired by the American writers Raymond Chandler and Dashiel Hammett, he created Nestor Burma, the Parisian private detective whose first mystery *120, rue de la Gare* was an instant success and marked the beginning of a new era in French detective fiction.

Over sixty novels were to follow over the next twenty years. Léo Malet won the 'Grand Prix de la Littérature policière' in 1947 and the 'Grand prix de l'humour noir' in 1958 for his series 'Les nouveaux mystères de Paris', each of which is set in a different *arrondissement*.

Léo Malet lives in Châtillon, just south of Paris.

Léo Malet

120 rue de la Gare
translated from the French by Peter Hudson
general editor: Barbara Bray

Pan Books
London, Sydney and Auckland

Published in France 1943 by S.E.P.E., Paris

This edition first published in Great Britain 1991 by

Pan Books Ltd, Cavaye Place, London SW10 9PG

9 8 7 6 5 4 3 2 1

ISBN 0 330 31322 3

Phototypeset by Input Typesetting Ltd, London
Printed in England by Clays Ltd, St Ives plc

Paris

Châtillon

OCCUPIED   ZONE

Château du Loir   La Ferté-Combettes

F R A N C E

Paray-le-Monial

Lyon

Nîmes   Marseille

0   miles   200
0   km   300

Contents

Prologue:
Germany 1940–1941

Ushering people in was just the job for Baptiste Cormier. He had the soul of a flunkey as well as a name like a butler.

But he'd lost some of his starch since he left his last situation, and at present he was lolling in the doorway, gazing dolefully at the ceiling and picking at a tooth with a spent match. Then suddenly he abandoned the mopping-up operation and straightened up.

'*Achtung!*' he shouted.

We all stopped talking, and with a scraping of benches and clatter of boots stood up and clicked our heels. The Aufnahme officer had just come on duty.

'At ease!' he said with a strong German accent, saluting and sitting down at the table that served him as a desk. We sat down too and went on with our conversations. There was still a good quarter of an hour till work was due to begin.

But after a few minutes spent sorting out papers the reception officer got up again and blew a loud blast on a whistle, indicating he had something to say to us. We stopped talking and turned to listen.

This time he spoke in German, then sat down again while the interpreter translated.

First came the usual instructions about the work, plus thanks for our efforts the previous day, when we'd registered a particularly large intake. He hoped that at this rate we'd be finished by tomorrow at the latest. As a reward each man was to be issued with a packet of tobacco.

Some awkward *Danke schöns* and stifled laughter greeted this pleasantry: we were to get what had earlier been confiscated from the chaps we were about to register.

At a sign from the interpreter, Cormier abandoned his teeth and opened the door.

'First twenty,' he called.

With a rattle of hobnailed boots a group detached itself from the crowd lined up in the hut and the day's work began.

The entry consisted of men who'd arrived from France a couple of days before. My job was to sit at one end of a table, extract certain information from each of the newcomers, put it down on a sheet of paper, then pass it along to the other eight *Schreibers*. When the paper and the person it referred to reached the other end of the table, the POW officiating there completed the form and appended a print of the subject's forefinger.

The dabs-taker was a young Belgian, and his task was lengthier if not more difficult than mine. At one point he asked me to slow down because he was getting submerged.

So I told Cormier not to send anyone to our table for a bit, and went outside to stretch my legs on the not-so-good earth.

It was July. The weather was fine. A warm sun shone on the barren landscape and a gentle southerly breeze was blowing. A sentry paced back and forth on his watchtower, his rifle barrel glinting in the sun.

I lit my pipe, and after a while went back to my table, puffing pleasantly. The Belgian had emerged from his traffic jam and we could get on.

I carefully sharpened my *ersatz* pencil, *Schreibstube* issue, with my knife, and took a fresh sheet of paper.

'Next gentleman, please,' I said, without looking up. 'Name?'

'I don't know.'

A low, expressionless voice.

I glanced at the speaker. A tall man with a gaunt but strong face, who must have been in his forties. His receding hair and bushy beard made a rather odd combination, and his left cheek was disfigured by an ugly scar. He was kneading his cap foolishly in remarkably slender hands, and looking at us all with a hangdog expression. On the lapels of his greatcoat he wore the red and black badge of the 6th Engineers.

'What do you mean – you "don't know"?'

'I don't know.'

'Isn't it in your papers?'

A vague gesture.

'Have you lost them?'

'Maybe. I don't know.'

'Haven't you any friends?'

He hesitated a moment. His jaw tensed.

'I . . . I don't know.'

A little man who looked like a crook, waiting his turn at another table, had been listening in on this strange conversation. He now came over and spoke to me.

'He's a tough nut, this one,' he said. He had the hoarse voice of a small-time hood, and enhanced the effect by speaking out of the corner of his mouth. 'Crafty sod's been making out he's crazy for more than a month. As good a wheeze as any, I suppose, to make them let him go.'

'Do you know him?'

'A bit . . . We both got put in the bag at the same time.'

'Where was that?'

'Château-du-Loir. I'm in the 6th Engineers.'

'Like him,' I said, pointing to the badge.

'Don't take any notice of that. Someone gave him that coat at Arvoures.'

'Do you know his name?'

'We call him the Blob. But I've never known his real name. We'd both been taken prisoner by the time we met, and he didn't have any papers – not even a newspaper in his pocket . . . It was like this. There were about ten of us in this little wood, and a chap just back from a recce had told us to watch out for Jerries. But to cut it short, we were caught like rats in a trap. The Germans were just taking us off to a farm where some more of our people were being held when we had to stop, near another wood. A bloke with his face all covered in blood was trying to crawl across the road. It was the Blob. He'd got his feet singed somewhere and they hurt him so much he couldn't walk. His eyes were out on stalks, and you should have seen his get-up!'

He started to laugh, giving his mouth an extra twist.

'It looked as if he'd been trying to give the Germans the slip by dressing in civvies. But he hadn't been able to lay his hands on the main items – the trousers and jacket – so he'd made do with just a shirt and tie! A real civvy shirt and tie, though, and there he was, wearing just them with his uniform on top. Either a real dope or dead clever. Whichever it was, he couldn't put one foot in front of the other, and the German guards made the two heftiest ones out of our lot carry him, first to the farm and then on to the camp. His feet were in a terrible state, and when they and the wound on his face had been looked after he stayed on with us. He never gave any trouble. He was quiet and polite and always said he couldn't remember anything pri . . . pre . . . some word meaning before.'

'Prior?'

'That's it – prior to being taken prisoner. What do you think of that? . . . Anyhow, good luck to him.'

'And he doesn't really belong to the 6th Engineers?'

'No – I told you, he was given that coat in the camp. There were plenty of chaps there from the regiment, and not one of us knew him.'

A conspiratorial wink.

'Well, as I say, he's a tough nut. Take it from Bébert. Bébert knows what he's talking about.'

'But how did he get this far in the condition he's in?'

'Ah!' drawled Bébert, as if to say 'That'd be telling!'

I stood up and took the man who'd forgotten his name by the arm. He didn't look to me as if he was shamming. The reception officer listened intently to what the interpreter said, then ran a monocled eye over the prisoner.

'Have him taken to hospital and kept under observation,' he ordered. 'The doctors will tell us if he's having us on.'

I took the man back to my table and filled in a pink form for him. It didn't take long – it was the briefest one I'd ever done. It just said, 'X. *Krank*. Amnesia.'

But as of now he had papers. And if he didn't have a name he did have a number. Henceforth he would be known as 60202.

I stood with my feet in the mud, leading against Hut 10A and thoughtfully smoking my pipe. In front of me stretched the main path through the camp, crossed in the middle by a dilapidated narrow-gauge railway line. Groups of men strolled about, picking their way round the puddles. Others leaned or sat in the doorways of the huts, smoking and chatting, their hands in their pockets or stuck in their belts. Strings of washing, hanging out to dry at the windows, flapped in the wind. The plaintive sound of a mouth organ drifted out from one of the huts. In the cheerful Sunday morning sunshine you might have taken it for a shanty town during the Gold Rush.

The doctor just coming off night duty in the infirmary was walking in my direction, escorted by an easy-going guard. He was on his way back to the hospital a couple of kilometres from the camp. According to his colleagues he was a very good surgeon. That made him, in the general opinion, a lousy doctor. When he drew level with me he stopped and spoke.

'My name's Hubert Dorcières,' he said as if we were in a fashionable Paris salon. 'And yours is Burma, if I'm not mistaken. About a year ago you got my sister out of a difficult situation. Saved her reputation, you might say. Do you remember?'

I remembered it very well. I also remembered that on the various occasions I'd needed to see him since I'd been in the camp, he'd just prescribed the usual pills, not deigning to mention we'd met before, even though he had my name in front of him in black and white.

I'd recognized him straight away, except for the beard. He'd been clean-shaven at the time his sister was being blackmailed. I remarked on this out of politeness; to seem to be taking an interest. I really didn't give a damn.

'Just a prisoner's whim,' said he, smiling and stroking the fringe of whiskers adorning his jaw. Then, lowering his voice conspiratorially: 'How is it a smart detective like you hasn't escaped yet?'

I said I hadn't had a holiday for ages, and prison was such a good substitute I didn't see the point of cutting it short. Also I was rather delicate, and the fresh air was good for my health. And between him and me, mightn't my talents come in useful to spot the leadswingers? And so on and so forth. Finally I brought the conversation round to the fact that the registration was finished for the time being, and I was out of a job for three weeks. Couldn't he get me into the hospital as an orderly?

He looked at me the way, in civilian life, he must have looked at a servant applying for a situation. I didn't care for it at all. In the end his thin lips uttered a vague acquiescence. He told me to come and see him next day in his office, and we shook hands and parted.

I knocked my pipe out on the wooden steps, scattering the ashes over some sparse tufts of heather. I then lit up again with a pinch of the Polish straw they sold in the canteen as tobacco. A stomach-churning dynamite, ideal for drowning the landscape in choking fumes.

Dr Hubert Dorcières might seem very polite, but when it came to actually doing you a favour you could whistle for it.

He took his time over my request, always supposing he bothered about it at all. I could have been sent out on a *Kommando* mission for all he cared. I'm not saying I'd have been any worse off, but I had a soft spot for barbed-wire fences, and derived a peculiar aesthetic satisfaction from seeing the sun set over the watchtowers.

Fortunately I did have a real friend at court. Paul Desiles was a doctor, too – short, fair, with curly hair and a pleasant square face. He got me a cushy job in the hospital in no time, and there I was able to catch several glimpses of No. 60202.

His condition was as puzzling as ever, but the medics, French and German, all agreed he wasn't shamming. However, they decided there was nothing they could do for him, and he was to be sent home in the next batch to be repatriated. Meanwhile he spent all his time sitting about twenty yards from the camp perimeter, propping his chin in his slender hands and staring into space more blankly than ever.

I tried several times to talk to him, but it was no good. Once, however, he did look at me with a flicker of interest.

'Haven't I seen you somewhere before?' he said.

'My name's Nestor Burma,' I told him, all agog at the thought of solving the mystery of the poor chap's identity. 'In civvy street I'm a private detective.'

'Nestor Burma,' he repeated. His tone had changed.

'That's right. Before the war I used to run the Fiat Lux Agency.'

'Nestor Burma . . . ' He'd turned pale, as though making a superhuman effort, and the scar on his face stood out. Then, with an infinitely weary shrug:

'No,' he murmured painfully. 'It doesn't mean anything to me.'

He lit a cigarette with a trembling hand and shuffled back to his post by the fence, looking out at the watchtower and the wood.

Days, weeks, months went by. Some of the badly wounded had already gone back to France. But 60202 was unlucky. His number had been included in the departure list, but at the last minute some careless pen-pusher forgot to copy it out, and for several more long weeks he was doomed to drag his misery round the well-kept paths of the hospital.

November came, and there was plenty of work to do. One day, when 60202 was staring into space as usual, I heard a typical Paris voice say:

'Good grief, hasn't the Blob gone home yet? A hard nut like him should have managed better than that!'

The speaker was just back from a *Kommando* mission. He was short, with a hoodlum's face, and spoke every word out of the corner of his mouth. He'd been injured in one hand, out on the working party.

'Bébert!' I exclaimed. 'How are you?'

'Could be better,' he growled, holding up his bandage.

'Only two fingers left and I damn near lost the whole fistful. Ah well . . . '

Not the type to look on the black side. He laughed out of the other corner of his mouth. A real contortionist.

'Let's hope it gets me sent home without having to put on an act, like his nibs.'

Sure enough, a few days later Bébert was released and went back to France on the December hospital train, with me and twelve hundred others. The man who'd lost his memory would have come too. Only for the past ten days he and his secret had been lying buried in the sandy earth by the little pine wood, swept by the wind from the sea.

One day I'd been away from the hospital, sent out with three other orderlies to collect a party of sick POWs from a *Kommando* some distance from the camp. When we got back I found 60202 had gone down with a fever. Neither Dorcières nor Desiles nor any of the other doctors could make out what was the matter with him.

For a week he hovered between life and death, then one Friday, when a gale was howling through the overhead wires and the rain pounded dismally down on the tin roofs, he suddenly, as they say, passed on.

I was on duty at the time. Everything was quiet in the ward apart from the racket going on outside. The patients were snoozing peacefully.

Then all of a sudden he called out.

'Burma!'

His voice was at the same time triumphant and harrowing.

I started. I could tell he knew at last what he was saying. I threw the rules to the winds, switched on the lights and went over to him. There was a gleam of intelligence in his eyes that I'd never seen there before.

'Hélène,' he said in a whisper. 'Tell Hélène – 120 rue de la Gare.'

Then he fell back, his brow covered in sweat, his teeth chattering and his face as pale as the sheet he was lying on.

'Paris?' I asked.

The light in his eyes grew brighter. He didn't answer, but he gave a feeble wave of assent. A moment later he was dead.

I just stood there for a while, at a loss. Then I noticed Bébert standing beside me. He'd been there all the time. Not that it had lasted long.

'Poor blighter,' he said. 'And I thought he was a phoney.'

Then a strange thing happened. Bébert's sentimentality put a stop to my own. Suddenly I was no longer just a POW bereft of individuality by the barbed wire. I was the real Nestor Burma again. Head of the Fiat Lux Agency. Dynamite Burma.

I was so glad to be my old self I went straight into action. I got an ink pad from the MO's empty office, brought it back into the ward and carefully took the dead man's fingerprints.

'Ugh!' Bébert spat out scornfully. 'Just like a cop!'

I laughed but said nothing, and switched the lights off.

Then, as I listened to the rain, I started to think. It wouldn't be a bad idea to ask the chaplain for a photograph of the deceased. Just to complete the file.

Part one
Lyon

1 The end of Bob Colomer

A dimmed light bulb shed a dull blue glow over the drowsing POWs.

The blacked-out train lurched and swayed blindly through towns and villages plunged in sleep. As it rushed through the darkness it threw up echoes from iron bridges, and sprinkled the fleecy white surface between the rails with fiery sparks.

We'd left Constance at midday and were now crossing snow-covered Switzerland. I was in a first-class compartment with five other ex-prisoners. Four of them were more or less asleep, their heads nodding on their chests. The fifth, a redhead by the name of Edouard, just sat opposite me and smoked.

We'd put up the folding table by the window, and on it, among the crusts left over from our numerous snacks, lay a couple of packets of tobacco. I helped myself from each, as the fancy took me. We were on our way to Neuchâtel, the last stop before the frontier.

I began to come out of my torpor to the sound of a military band that seemed to burst forth right inside our compartment. Four of my companions were jostling each other by the door leading into the corridor. Edouard was yawning. The train was still moving, but only slowly. There was a lot of smoke and steam and hissing and shouting. A sudden jolt brought me half-awake. I tried to stand up, and another lurch landed me on Ginger opposite. The header I gave him in the chest brought me completely back to my senses.

The train had come to a halt.

The vast station was filled with attar of soot. Among the sizeable crowd on the platform, young women from the Red Cross bustled to and fro. There was a guard of honour to greet us: I could see their bayonets gleaming in the meagre light. Farther off, a brass band was playing the 'Marseillaise'.

We'd arrived in Lyon. Lyon-Perrache station, to be precise. It was two o'clock by my watch and I had a nasty taste in my mouth. The tobacco we'd got in Zurich, the chocolate and sausages and coffee we'd acquired in Neuchâtel, some sparkling wine from Bellegarde and various kinds of fruit from all over the place, presented my digestion with a puzzle that could only be solved outside my innards.

'How long do we stop here, sweetie?' I asked one of the charming young ladies with a nose rather too sharp for my taste. She was writing down the addresses of ex-POWs, anxious to speed the good news of their release to their nearest and dearest.

'An hour,' she said.

Edouard lit another cigarette and gave me a wink.

'I know Perrache station like the back of my hand,' he said. He then climbed down on to the platform and disappeared past the left-luggage office.

He really did know his way around: he came back half an hour later with a couple of bottles of wine in his overcoat pockets. Pals in these parts, he said.

The wine wasn't bad. It didn't taste any worse than the Polish tobacco. But perhaps that was because I'd got out of the habit. The trouble was, what with that and the sparkling Bellegarde, we started to feel very affectionate towards the feminine element around us.

One in particular was bareheaded, tall and slim, and stood apart from the rest with her hands thrust deep in the pockets of a fawn trenchcoat. She looked strangely alone, as if lost in her own thoughts, there by the newspaper stall under a flickering lamp. Her pale oval face, with its wistful expression and eyes bright as if from weeping, was curiously disturbing. The bitter December wind played in her hair.

She looked about twenty – one of those mysterious women you see only on railway stations: night fantasies which appear to the imagination of tired travellers and disappear with the darkness that gave them birth.

Edouard and I both noticed her at the same time.

'Phew, that's a pretty girl!' he said with an admiring whistle.

Then he chuckled.

'It sounds silly, but I think I've seen her before somewhere.'

Not all that silly. I had the same feeling.

Under the ginger thatch that hadn't seen a comb for four days, Edouard's brow was furrowed in thought. Then his eyes lit up and he gave me a triumphant dig in the ribs.

'I've got it!' he exclaimed. 'I knew I'd seen her somewhere. It was at the pictures! Don't you recognize her? She's Michèle Hogan, the film star!'

There was a certain resemblance. The girl in the trenchcoat certainly wasn't the actress who'd starred in *The Storm*, but she was sufficiently like her to have struck me for a moment as familiar.

'I'm going to ask for her autograph,' said Edouard, who had no doubts on the subject. 'She can't refuse an ex-POW.'

He made his way down the corridor, but the guard wouldn't let him get off: the train was just about to leave.

It was then I saw someone I'd have recognized anywhere hurry on to the platform. He wore a light-coloured sports cap and a camel-hair coat, and was shouldering his way along as if against some obstacle. No doubt about it – it was Robert Colomer, once of the Fiat Lux Agency, my own Bob, as he'd come to be called in the bars on the Champs-Elysées.

I shoved the window down and yelled and waved my arms.

'Colo! Hi, Colo!'

He turned his rather sinister face towards me, but apparently either didn't see or didn't recognize me. Had I changed so much?

'Bob!' I shouted. 'Colomer! Don't you remember your friends any more? It's Burma – Nestor Burma – just back from the country!'

He was standing next to one of the Red Cross ladies, and he now let out a resounding oath and elbowed her out of the way.

'Burma!' he gasped. 'What luck! Get out, for God's sake – get out! I've discovered something really important . . .'

The train had started to pull out. The ex-prisoners were at the windows, waving their caps. The general din was suddenly swamped by another burst of the 'Marseillaise'. Colomer had jumped on the running board and was hanging on with both hands to the window of my compartment. Then suddenly his face convulsed as if in terrible pain.

'Boss!' he cried. 'Boss! . . . 120 rue de la Gare . . .'

Then he let go and crashed down on to the platform.

I hurtled to the end of the carriage, socked the guard who tried to stop me, opened the door and jumped out. The door swung to, catching a corner of my coat, and for a second I thought I was going to be dragged under the wheels. I was pulled along the platform, every fibre of me in pain, my ears filled as if in a dream by the shrieks of terrified women. Then a soldier from the guard of honour rushed forward and freed my coat with a stroke of his bayonet. I lay there looking up at the iron girders in the station roof, unable to get to my feet.

'Good God, he's drunk!' said some man in uniform.

I was surrounded by a chattering crowd. I scrutinized them as best I could. Not that I was looking for anyone in particular. I just wanted to make sure I could still see straight and hadn't been the victim of a delusion.

For as Colomer hit the ground I'd seen quite clearly that the back of his coat had a bullet hole in it. And just opposite, close to the newspaper stall, something metallic had glinted in the faint flicker of the lamp. That something was held in the ungloved hand of a strange girl wearing a trenchcoat.

2 *Night conversation*

I was just aware enough of what was happening to realize I was being put on a stretcher and shoved in the back of an ambulance. The smell of disinfectant and poor quality petrol made me feel sick.

Soon I was lying on a reasonably white hospital bed, being examined by a pink-faced doctor. He was a corpulent, jovial type, and called me a drunk when he caught the reek of wine on my breath. Then he made a few far-fetched jokes about POWs and assured me that the bruising wasn't serious. It would soon disappear with a bit of massage and I'd be able to start my acrobatics again if I liked. He reminded me how much I owed the soldier from the guard of honour. I didn't doubt it for a moment.

The nurse who put the dressings on wasn't young. She wasn't pretty either. I know that kind of nurse is the most efficient, but as my condition wasn't desperate they might have given me the benefit of a beauty queen.

Anyway, I didn't have long to worry about it. Everyone went off and I was left in semi-darkness. Despite a certain amount of discomfort, I decided against the pain-killers they'd left on the night table. I wanted to think.

I didn't have much time for that either. I heard a distant town clock strike four, and shortly afterwards the nurse came back with a man pushing a trolley. They loaded me on to it and I had an unpleasant journey down gloomy, deserted corridors, ending in a brightly lit room. I blinked like a disturbed owl. I didn't need surgery. Why take me to an operating theatre? When I lifted my head and looked around the answer became clear.

The doctor was there, but he wasn't alone. Two men were with him, both dressed in beige raincoats and iron-grey trilbies. You'd have sworn they were brothers. Some brothers. The redder-faced of the two came over to me.

'How are you feeling?' he said. A careful shave and casual manner offset the fiery face and regulation gaberdine, and he looked rather out of the common. I noticed he was wearing evening dress underneath the coat. He obviously belonged to the anti-gambling squad. Either that or his social life had been interrupted on my account.

'The doctor says I can ask you a few questions. Do you feel up to it?'

What courtesy! I nearly had a fit and lost consciousness. Yes, he could go ahead.

'A man was shot at Perrache station last night,' he began. 'The one hanging on to the window of your carriage. No point in asking if you knew him, eh? We found a Fiat Lux Agency card on him. And when we came here to put a few questions to the ex-POW who'd jumped off the train, we discovered he was none other than the director of the Agency. That's you, isn't it?'

'Yes. You might almost say I'm a colleague of yours.'

'Yes . . . Well. . . . My name's Bernier. Commissaire Armand Bernier.'

'Pleased to meet you. You'll know my name already. Is Bob dead?'

'Bob? . . . Oh, Colomer! Yes. Riddled with .32 bullets. What was he saying to you when he was shot?'

'Nothing special. Just that he was pleased to see me.'

'Had you arranged to meet? I mean – did he know you were coming back and passing through Lyon?'

'Of course,' I said sarcastically. 'The camp authorities gave me special permission to send him a telegram.'

'Let's not be flippant, Monsieur Burma. You do understand I'm trying to catch the man who killed your employee, don't you?'

'Colleague.'

'What? As you like. So you met by chance?'

'Yes. Complete coincidence. I noticed him on the platform and called him. God knows he was the last person I expected to see there at two in the morning. Took him a hell of a long time to recognize me, though. I must have put on weight. Anyway, he seemed overjoyed to see me, and jumped up on to the running board. There was a fair amount of noise in the station and I didn't hear the shots. But I saw the expression of disbelief on his face. Then, when he rolled over on the platform, I noticed his raincoat was all torn at the back. Pity – it was rather a nice one.'

'Any idea who did it?'

'No. It's a mystery to me, Commissaire. I'm only just back from POW camp and . . .'

'Quite, quite. When was the last time you saw him?'

'At the beginning of the war. I closed the agency and joined up. Colomer must have gone on working on his own account.'

'Wasn't he called up?'

'No. Unfit for active service. Bit frail. Something to do with his lungs . . .'

'Did you stay in touch?'

'A card from time to time. Then I was taken prisoner.'

'Was he interested in politics?'

'Not before September 1939.'

'But since?'

'Since, I don't know. I'd be very surprised.'

'Was he well off?'

'Don't make me laugh.'

'Broke?'

'Yes. He did manage to put a bit away once. But a few years ago his bank manager hopped it with the money. After that he spent as he earned; lived from hand to mouth.'

'We found several thousand francs on him. New notes mostly. I was a bit surprised . . . '

'You and me both,' I said.

Commissaire Bernier nodded.

'Why did you jump off the train?' he asked quietly.

I began to laugh.

'That's the first silly question you've asked,' I said.

'Answer it anyway,' he said, unruffled.

'It was a shock, seeing my assistant gunned down right in front of me. Some welcome home . . . I wanted to know what it was all about.'

'And . . . ?'

'And then I fell flat on my face.'

'Had you noticed anything out of the way before it happened?'

'Nothing at all.'

'And you didn't see the flash when the gun went off?'

'I didn't hear anything and I didn't see anything. It all happened so fast. I couldn't even tell you whereabouts we were in the station. The train was moving . . . That's going to make it difficult to determine the angle of fire,' I added carelessly.

'Oh, we're already clear on that point,' he said. 'The killer must have been by the paper stall, under the lamp. It's a miracle no one else was hurt. An extremely good marksman, if you want my opinion.'

'So that rules out the possibility that he was aiming at me and killed Colomer by mistake.'

'Aiming at you? Good Lord, I'd never thought of that!'

'Keep it that way,' I said. 'I'm only trying to exercise the old grey matter. We mustn't overlook anything, and quite a few people do have it in for me. Still, they're not clever enough to have known in advance when I was going to be released.'

'That's true. But what you say opens up new possibilities. So Robert Colomer was more a colleague than an employee?'

'Yes. We were collaborators. Partners in crime, you might say.'

'Supposing some crook you had put away decided to get his own back . . . ?'

'I suppose it's within the bounds of possibility,' I lied.

The doctor was beginning to show signs of impatience. The Commissaire glanced towards him.

'I've kept you long enough, Monsieur Burma,' he said. 'I won't take up much more of your time. But I'll need the names of the most dangerous criminals you've helped to gaol in the last few years. Men who wouldn't balk at murder.'

I said that after what had happened at Perrache my brain didn't feel up to it, but if he'd let me have a few hours' rest . . .

'By all means,' he answered cordially. 'Whatever you say. I can't ask the impossible. You've already made a great effort. Thank you.'

'I'm afraid I haven't been all that useful,' I said. 'I've spent the past seven months somewhere between Bremen and Hamburg, and even with my well-known flair I couldn't tell what my colleague was up to a few hundred miles away.'

He shook hands and wished me a speedy recovery. He also shook hands with the doctor, who by this time had lost much of his joviality and muttered an inaudible good-bye. The Commissaire and his silent associate then left.

I was relieved to escape from the harsh light of the operating theatre and get back to my primitive couch. The nurse, who still wasn't a beauty queen, tucked me in. I swallowed a sleeping pill and went to sleep.

3 Colomer's curious taste in books

The day after Bernier's visit the doctor decided I was well enough to be transferred to an annexe on the other side of the street. Here a handful of repatriated POWs, all more or less the worse for their experiences, wandered about at their own sweet will, waiting to be allowed to go home. I was given a massage by a kind of gorilla, who then wrapped me up in cold sheets and handed me over to a nurse with much the same sex appeal as her colleague over the road.

However, she turned out to be helpfulness personified, and agreed to post four letters and an interzone card for me. The train I had leaped from so dramatically was due to drop the other POWs off at Montpellier, Sète, Béziers and Castelnaudary. I'd written to Edouard at the military hospital in each of these places, asking him to send me the suitcase I left in the luggage rack as quickly as he could. The interzone card was for my concierge.

At midday, just as my neighbour was preparing to make a hat out of his newspaper, I asked him to let me have a look at it. He was deaf, so I had to shout.

At the bottom of the back page, under 'Stop Press', there was a brief account of the bloody events which had greeted my arrival.

TRAGEDY AT PERRACHE STATION:
Last night, as a hospital train was leaving Lyon-Perrache station carrying repatriated POWs on their way to convalesce in the south, M. Robert Colomer, aged 35, formerly of Paris but recently living in Lyon at 40 rue de la Monnaie, was shot down while in conversation with one of the ex-prisoners.

The victim, later identified as a private detective from the Fiat Lux agency run by the celebrated 'Dynamite Burma', died instantly.

His pockets contained no clues that might help the police in their investigations.

An immediate on-the-spot search produced disappointing results. The police detained a known political agitator supposed to be under house arrest, but he turned out to be unarmed.

The murder weapon – a revolver – could not be found either at the scene of the crime or in the area around the station. . . .

The final paragraph was given up to my accident, which the reporter greatly deplored. My name wasn't mentioned.

In the afternoon, just as the time was beginning to drag, Commissaire Bernier burst in. He was accompanied by his taciturn colleague, who took a few notes without opening his mouth.

Bernier had brought some photographs of Colomer for me to identify. When I'd done that I gave him three names: Jean Figaret, Joseph Villebrun and Désiré Mailloche, known as 'Dédé the Pigalle Hyena'. They were the toughest thugs Bob and I had helped to put behind bars. In the normal course of events Villebrun, a bank robber, should have been freed from Nîmes prison the previous October.

The Commisssaire thanked me, and I told him I was glad to see my name wasn't mentioned, though that must only be because the journalist had to rush to meet his deadline. I said I hoped it would continue to be omitted – I needed some rest. He assured me that if it was up to him no one would take the slightest notice of me. Then the two policemen left.

The man in the next bed might have been deaf but he wasn't blind. He inquired solicitously what the coppers wanted with me. I told him I'd cut a bailiff to pieces, and this had given me a headache and a lot of other problems. But Greta Garbo would soon get me out of trouble.

I yelled all this at the top of my voice, so my deaf neighbour wasn't the only one in the ward to stare at me anxiously. Imprisonment had a strange effect on some people.

Once I was suspected of being touched I was left in peace. No one spoke another word to me, and I took advantage of the lull to continue my meditation on the movies and the case of Michèle Hogan's double. The one who'd been holding a black automatic in her white hand when Colomer collapsed.

Was it a .32?

I had no means of knowing, but like a fool I kept turning the question over in my mind until the nurse brought me the evening paper. All it said was that Colomer's place had been searched but no clues were found among his effects. His trunk was full of detective novels.

I spent two days in bed and on the third I was as right as rain. Mae West herself wouldn't have daunted me. In order to get permission to go into town, I went to a poorly heated office where two blonde typists were testing new makes of lipstick under the indulgent eye of a bespectacled clerk.

My dear old nanny came from Lyon, I explained, and I wanted to go and have a look at her native city, especially as it was such a fine day. Or rather as there was slightly less fog than usual.

They weren't hard to please in that office, and I soon got what I wanted.

My uniform had already been threadbare, what with first the war and then the prison camp. My fall from the train was the last straw, so it had been replaced by the standard khaki demob outfit. It might have been made to measure, give or take a few inches.

So this was what I was wearing as I made my way towards the Place Bellecour. My nanny wasn't from Lyon, for the very good reason that I'd never had one. And I had no need to visit the town as I'd got to know it quite well enough when I was twenty or so and had been on my uppers there.

I felt quite nostalgic when I saw the avenue de la République again, with its little covered passageways leading off near Carnot's statue, one of them the original home of the 'guignol' puppet show. Somewhere around here I was once ignominiously chucked out of a bar because I'd had an egg-nog and not enough money to pay for it.

I smoked my pipe as I walked along looking for the bar . . . if it still existed.

I was so lucky it was quite upsetting. First I saw the *Crépuscule* on a book-stall. So the paper had moved from Paris to Lyon. I bought a copy to see whether Marc Covet had come with it. Yes. There was my friend's name on a typically woolly article on page two. Then I found the café. The name hadn't changed, nor had the décor, nor had the owner. Probably even the dust was still the same: it had an antique look about it. And finally, perched on a high stool at the bar, I saw Marc Covet himself, playing poker dice with another reporter. His nose was as red and his eyes as watery as ever.

I put my hand on his shoulder and he turned and let out an exclamation of surprise. Before he had time to speak I said meaningly:

'So you don't recognize old Roly, eh?'

'Roly?' he said slowly. 'Oh yes – Roly Stone!'

He burst out laughing and put the dice back in their cup on the counter.

'I'm chucking it in,' he said to his opponent. 'This is an old pal of mine. Must have a word with him. Let's say you won.'

He led me to a secluded table in a corner of the room.

'What'll it be?' he said.

'Fruit juice.'

'Mine's a beer.'

A nonchalant waiter (not the one who'd thrown me out some years before) brought us our drinks. Covet pointed at my glass.

'Colo's death must have shaken you up,' he said.

'It's because there's no more absinthe,' I replied. 'But you're right – it has upset me. You know it was me he was talking to when he was shot.'

He thumped the table and swore.

'So it was you who—?'

'Yes. Me again. Practising a circus turn. But keep it to yourself.'

'You don't think I'd pass it on to a rival, do you?'

'Don't be daft, Marc. I mean nobody must know – not anyone on the other papers, no one. This is strictly between ourselves. Later on we'll see.'

His pen was obviously itching already, but he promised with a fairly good grace to hold off. Once that was out of the way I said:

'Did you see much of Colomer lately?'

'We met now and again.'

'What was he doing with himself?'

'I've no idea. He didn't seem too well off.'

'Did he try to touch you?'

'No. But he was living in—'

'The rue de la Monnaie. I know. Not a very high-class neighbourhood. But that doesn't mean anything. Was he still working as a detective?'

'I've told you, I don't know anything about him. We were just acquaintances. Can't have seen each other more than four times in the last six months.'

'Do you know what sort of people he mixed with?'

'No. I always saw him alone.'

'No girl-friend?'

'Er, well, funny you should mention that. No girl-friend, no. But talking of women—'

'Well?'

'You knew him better than I did. Wasn't he a bit odd?'

'What makes you think that?'

'He came to see me at work a little while ago. He wanted a list of books about the Marquis de Sade. A catalogue of his works and so on. Asked if there was a biography. I didn't know the Marquis de Sade had written anything at all. Colomer explained . . . Don't look at me like that, Burma. Culture's not my strong point.'

'All right – we can talk about culture another day. Did you say you'd get him the list he wanted?'

'Yes. When I chivvied him about what he was going to do with it, he said he needed it for some research. That made me laugh.'

'I don't doubt it. And then?'

'I asked our literary critic to help me out. He said my friend – he obviously thought it was really me – wouldn't find Sade's own works in the ordinary public library because they're banned. But he suggested two or three other books he could consult. And now all the typists think I'm some sort of a maniac. As you can imagine, the critic soon put them in the picture, and—'

'Spare me the speech about your reputation,' I interrupted. 'It's never been up to much, and this little incident won't make it any worse. Do you remember the titles of the books?'

'What! Not you too?'

'Do you remember the titles?'

'No. I—'

'Listen, Marc. Eventually there'll be a terrific story for you in all this. But you must help me first. Both the titles and the authors' names could be useful.'

'This'll finish off my reputation for good,' he groaned. 'You want me to go back to the critic again?'

'Yes. Tonight. Do your best to get me all the dope.'

'All right then, if you say so. So long as I get priority when the story breaks. But look,' he chuckled, 'are you sure imprisonment hasn't turned your brain?'

'Absolutely sure. Though not everyone would agree.'

I clapped my hands to attract the waiter's attention. 'Same again,' I said.

When we'd been served I looked Marc Covet straight in the eye.

'Do you remember Hélène Chatelain?' I asked.

'Your typist-cum-secretary-cum-colleague?'

'Yes. What's become of her?'

'Well, after you left for the army I got her a job on *Lectout*, the Readall Press Agency. I thought you knew.'

'I knew about that. But afterwards?'

'She's still there. They went to Marseille during the 1940 exodus, but they're back in Paris now.'

'You've never seen Hélène in these parts?'

'No. Why?'

'No special reason. Now let's go to your place. We're about the same size. I want to borrow a suit. I can't stand the sight of any more khaki.'

I paid and we left. It was cold outside, with the kind of fog that goes right through your clothes, so we walked at a good pace. Covet grumbled when I stopped in front of a stationer's to look at some postcards on a revolving stand.

I took no notice of his protests and went inside. When I came out again I was carrying their best photo of Michèle Hogan.

'Beautiful girl, eh?' I said. I took out my trusty little scissors and cut off the part of the card with the actress's name on it. 'What's become of her in all this upheaval?'

'Hollywood,' he snorted. 'You interested in her? Your mistress, perhaps?'

'No. My daughter.'

Organized chaos reigned in the reporter's room. He dived into it and held out a check three-piece which I liked but refused. I finally chose an innocuous grey suit that made me look like a confidential clerk.

'Give me an overcoat or a raincoat,' I said, preening in front of the mirror. 'I don't need a hat. My beret will do.'

'Will that be all?' he inquired. 'Sure I can't lend you my razor? Polish your shoes? Give you my ration cards and my girl-friend's address?'

'Another time,' I said. 'See you tonight. Be sure you get me the stuff on the sadist.'

4 The ghost of Eiffel Tower Joe

40 rue de la Monnaie was a third-class hotel (rooms by the month or the day), but clean. It was run by an ex-boxer who sat smoking his pipe by a meagre fire and listening sceptically to an Arab's tale of woe. The man was probably asking for more time to pay the rent.

When the North African had vanished I introduced myself as a member of Colomer's family, grief-stricken at his sudden and inexplicable death.

We'd been separated by the war and I'd just arrived in Lyon when . . . And so on and so forth. A home-grown cock and bull story, punctuated by sniffs in the right places.

Whether the hotelier believed it or not, he launched into a panegyric on the deceased. A likeable young man: clean and polite, and paid regularly. Not like these bloody wogs, etc., etc.

'A detective? Perhaps, if that's what the papers say. But he didn't look like one. Kept it under his hat. I suppose that's part of the job!'

He began to laugh and then suddenly stopped. Hilarity wasn't quite the thing in the presence of the bereaved.

'And his fiancée?' I said. 'Have you seen her lately?'

'Fiancée? Was he engaged?'

'Yes. To a very fine girl. She'll be devastated when she hears about this. If she doesn't know already. She used to live in Marseille, but she left there some time ago. I thought she'd come here to join Robert. Look, here's her photo. You say you've never seen her?'

'No, never. Hey, what a beautiful girl!'

'You said it. Poor Robert.'

I went on to his sister. She'd come to see him recently, hadn't she? She hadn't? Oh! I must have been mistaken. It must have been her other brother she'd visited. Oh, yes, it was a big family. I asked a few other trivial questions. The answers were equally uninteresting and told me nothing. Had no mail arrived since the er . . . um . . . event? Here a choked sob. No, Monsieur Colomer didn't receive many letters. An interzone card from his parents now and again.

I left the hotel and crossed the river to the Palais de Justice. Luckily Commissaire Bernier was there, and I was ushered into his gloomy office.

'Hello,' he said cheerfully. 'Back on your feet, eh? How are you feeling? You do look smart! I'll shake your hand gently. I wouldn't want you to fall to pieces.'

'You don't have to worry,' I answered. 'I'm completely recovered. Tough, that's me. How's the investigation going?'

He offered me a rickety chair (it must have been the one he used for interrogating difficult customers), followed by a Gauloise which I refused (I prefer my pipe). He lit his cigarette and my pipe with a lighter much the worse for wear, then said:

'I can be frank with you, can't I?' – as though I was naïve enough to believe him. 'Well, we're all at sea. I apologize for not keeping you informed, but we're up to our eyes in work. Your colleague certainly kept himself to himself. We've found out practically nothing about him. As for Villebrun, the bank robber, he came out of prison in Nîmes about the time you said, but there's no trace of him after that. We've located one of his old gang here in Lyon. But it wasn't him that shot Colomer. He's got an alibi.'

'Oh! alibis—'

'This one holds water. He was arrested for pickpocketing about ten hours before the crime. Caught red-handed.'

'I see what you mean.'

'Of course, we've questioned him. He maintains he hasn't seen his boss since he went to prison. We're checking on it.'

He threw his cigarette butt in the direction of the stove.

'By the way,' he said, after a pause, 'we know what your man Colomer was up to at the station when disaster struck.'

'Oh?'

'He was about to slope off into the occupied zone.'

'Slope off? That's a funny way to put it.'

'Everything goes to show he was in a great hurry to leave. Afraid of something? He didn't tell his landlord he was going, he didn't have any luggage. You didn't see a suitcase, did you?'

'No, that's true.'

'So, no luggage. He didn't have a pass either, but his wallet was well lined. As I told you before, it contained several thousand francs . . . Nine thousand to be exact. He'd just picked it up. Since the influx of people from the occupied zone there's been a shortage of accommodation here, so Colomer had to take a room in a third-class hotel in a street where it wasn't wise to carry large sums of money on you. So he'd left all this cash with a lawyer. And when he heard what had happened, Maître Montbrison came forward—'

'Julien Montbrison, do you mean?'

'Yes. You know him?'

'Slightly. I didn't know he was in Lyon.'

'Some detective you are,' he chuckled. 'He's lived here for years.'

'It isn't my job to keep track of lawyers' comings and goings,' I retorted. 'Could you give me his address?'

He leafed through the statements.

'26 rue Alfred-Jarry.'

'Thanks. I feel a bit lonely. I think I'll pay him a call. I hope he still has a good cellar?'

'How should I know, Monsieur Burma?' he said, nettled.

'Very sorry,' I said with a laugh. 'You were saying?'

'What?'

'Montbrison's statement.'

'Oh yes. Well, it's quite instructive. It says your man Bob went to see him the night he was killed and took out all his money. At eleven o'clock at night.'

'Odd time to collect money.'

'Exactly. It shows he needed the cash to cross the line in a hurry. I'll prove it to you in a minute. Montbrison was at a party, and when he got back Colomer was waiting for him. Before that, he'd done the rounds of all the places where the lawyer was likely to be. All the places except the right one, of course. When he'd had enough he went back and waited for him at home. According to Montbrison he seemed very agitated. He was so nervous Montbrison asked him a few questions. But he refused to answer. Just insisted on reclaiming every centime of his money. He didn't say anything about a journey, but he certainly intended to leave. I'd say run away, given his behaviour. He must have been in some danger he'd only found out about late that afternoon. (His first visit to Montbrison's house was at about seven.) And he must have been fleeing not only Lyon but the unoccupied zone itself. He claimed his money to pay for the illegal crossing. (You may not know it, just coming out of POW camp, but that's a pretty expensive operation.) We found the proof in the lining of his overcoat. It had slipped through a hole in his pocket. Two single tickets for St. Deniaud, a village not far from Paray-le-

Monial on the border. It's also known as The Colander.
No need to explain why.'

'I see. Two tickets, you say?'

'Yes. Does that suggest anything to you?'

'No, but it's odd.'

'Not really. Only one of the tickets had been clipped,
and they were bought a few minutes apart. It must have
happened something like this. Colomer bought the first
ticket, but mislaid it through the hole in his pocket before
it was clipped. Being so on edge, he assumed he must have
dropped it. So he went back and bought another one, which
he kept in his hand till it was clipped. Then he put it in
the same pocket, where it too fell through the lining. That's
the only explanation, unless you like the theory of a travelling companion who did him in.'

'Rather improbable. If Bob was as frightened as you say,
he wouldn't have run away with the person who'd scared
him. Anyhow, he wouldn't have been so obliging as to pay
for his killer's ticket. Of course you've taken prints?'

'Yes. They're all Colomer's.'

'And does all this get you anywhere?'

'No stone must be left unturned,' he replied.

'Excellent principle. Perhaps you'd let me apply it and
look through the papers he was carrying. I knew him better
than you did, and—'

'And it's possible that something which seems quite insignificant to me might give you a clue?'

'Exactly.'

He got up and issued a brief order through the internal
telephone. Then he hung up again and said abruptly:

'What was your impression of Colomer?'

'He wasn't exactly distraught, but now I come to think
of it he did look strange. As if he was rather worked up –
that's it. And as if he was relieved to see me there.'

'What did he say?'

'That he was pleased to see me. That's all. But you're right, Commissaire. Maybe it wasn't just because he was glad I was free.'

A uniformed policeman knocked and came in with the contents of my ex-agent's pockets. I glanced through his identity papers, the agency card, his ration book and a lot of other bits and pieces. No reference anywhere to 120, rue de la Gare. I examined the two rail tickets. Only one was perforated. There were a few interzone postcards, all from Bob's parents. They'd stayed put in the Paris suburbs, and complained that times were difficult. Their spelling was shaky.

'Lukily,' said the most recent card, 'your fathers found work as nite watchman at the soc. for edmin and distribution. Were fine.' Etc.

I'd have to go and see the old couple when I got back to Paris, and offer them my condolences. A lousy task that I didn't at all relish.

I noted down the address: Villa les Iris, rue Raoul-Ubac, Chatillon.

'Found something?' Bernier asked, his eyes lighting up.

I explained, and the light went out.

'It's just like all this', he grumbled, pointing to a bunch of yellowing newspaper cuttings. 'Might be of some use to us if the bloke wasn't dead.'

'Colomer, you mean?'

'No. Georges Parris, the international pearl thief. You know – Eiffel Tower Joe.'

Yes, I knew. I'd had the honour of laying a trap for Parris, and the pleasure of seeing him fall into it. He was a lover of puns, riddles, crosswords and other childish amusements, who signed his letters with a sketch of the Eiffel Tower. But the elegant and cultivated jewel thief hadn't rotted in prison. He had a remarkable talent for walking through walls. But you couldn't accuse the French prison system of negligence. Eiffel Tower Joe had escaped in similar fashion from gaols in London, Vienna and New York. He'd drowned while out swimming in England early in 1938, and his body was found half-eaten by crabs on a beach in Cornwall. He'd been having a holiday under a false name between two jobs. Jewellers and police forces throughout the world had heaved a sigh of relief.

But why had Colomer needed to look into this ancient history? I read the local press cuttings carefully.

'Do they open up any new possibilities?' asked the Commisssaire as I was folding them up.

'None. But anyhow, this is one crime Eiffel Tower Joe isn't guilty of.' I tapped a photo of the dead crook in one of the cuttings.

'You never can tell,' said the Commissaire with a smile. 'Lyon is full of spiritualists, theosophists and miracle workers. A ghost wouldn't be so extraordinary!'

It was growing late. I got up from the creaking chair.

'I dropped in at the rue de la Monnaie before I came here,' I said. 'Just to sniff around. I didn't find anything special. I could have kept quiet about it, but I was pretty sure the owner of the hotel would tell you. So don't waste time going off on a wild-goose chase. I pretended I was one of Bob's relations, and dragged in his fiancée, his sister, his aunt, and how he had measles when he was a little boy. And so on. No good. The owner of the hotel was talkative enough, but he didn't really seem to know anything.'

'Thanks for telling me,' said the Commissaire as he showed me out. 'It's best for us not to keep any secrets from one another.'

I gravely agreed.

But as I went down the clammy stairs I was strongly tempted to laugh.

5 Information about Colomer

I asked three natives I ran into in the fog how to get to the rue Alfred-Jarry from the Place Bellecour, then made my way thoughtfully towards the solicitor's house.

Colomer had suddenly needed to go to Paris. So much so that he'd tried to cross the demarcation line illegally. He'd bought two tickets for St. Whatsitsname. Why? Probably because the person who was supposed to go with him was already in the station. Perhaps had come in on another train. Who was this person? The girl in the trenchcoat? The murderer? If I'd really seen what I thought I'd seen, they were one and the same person. Of course, I'd told Bernier it seemed unlikely Colomer would have bought his murderer a ticket, but that was part of our policy of mutual frankness. Otherwise known as bunkum.

My objection would have made sense if what I'd seen of Colomer had corresponded at all to the Commissaire's description. But was Colomer in a state of panic? I'd seen him only for a few seconds, but I could deny that categorically. He was excited certainly, but he'd shown no trace of fear. And when he was hit his face had expressed nothing but painful surprise. He hadn't been expecting it.

Be that as it may, his destination was 120 rue de la Gare, the mysterious address murmured under equally dramatic circumstances by the POW who'd lost his memory. What was the relationship between the two men? And between the rue de la Gare in the 19th arrondissement of Paris and the rue de la Monnaie in Lyon, both in the Arab quarter of their respective cities? At this point in my cogitations I stepped on the foot of a passer-by, and not wanting to inflict useless suffering I asked him the way to the rue Alfred-Jarry. He told me I was in it.

Number 26 looked prosperous, and so did its ground floor tenant, as I observed when a taciturn and sickly looking manservant led me into an enormous office where his employer was waiting for me, smoking a cigarette.

Julien Montbrison didn't seem to be suffering unduly from the rationing. He was plump and jovial, just as I'd known him in Paris several years before. It was a pleasing plumpness, without a hint of vulgarity. Despite his corpulence he looked elegant and distinguished. The only false note was struck by all the rings on his fingers. He had a parvenu's love of flashy jewellery. Today, for example, he was wearing a gold signet ring set with three brilliants, one of which didn't match the others and made an expensive piece look like something from a bazaar. But this was a trivial weakness that in no way detracted from the man's talent. He was clever, wily, eloquent and cynical, and, as I knew from experience (we'd downed a number of glasses together), an agreeable companion.

When I came in he closed the book he was reading – a handsome edition of the works of Edgar Allan Poe – and came towards me, his pudgy hand extended and a charming smile on his face.

'Burma,' he cried. 'What a splendid surprise! What are you doing in Lyon?'

I told him while he cleared a chair of several hefty law books. Then I sat down and told him at his request about my experiences as a POW.

On the whole, people don't give a damn about your

experiences as a POW, though they think it polite to appear to sympathize with your afflictions, as they call them.

After going through the usual motions and turning out some frightful platitudes, I got to the point.

'Good Lord,' he exclaimed. 'I knew Colomer had been killed, but I didn't know you were a witness to the murder. Not a very agreeable return to civilian life.'

He stubbed his cigarette out in the ash tray.

'No. It could have been better,' I agreed.

He held out an expensive gold cigarette case.

'Have one. You won't find them anywhere else. Philip Morris. I've got a little stock.'

'Extremely rare. But if you don't mind, I'm not a connoisseur, and I prefer my pipe.'

'Ah! The famous old briar. As you wish.'

He lit my pipe and his cigarette.

'To get back to Colomer,' he said, exhaling a pungent cloud of smoke, 'has our brilliant detective any ideas on the subject?'

'No. None. I've been rather out of touch. But the police think Bob's death was a gangland killing. Either for political reasons or in some other connection. And what you told them seems to confirm it.'

'Oh, so you know about that?'

'Up to a point. I know Colomer came here just a few hours before he was shot.'

'Yes. To collect the money he'd left in my keeping—'

'Just a moment. Where did it come from? I've heard eight or nine thousand francs mentioned. That's a lot of money. I mean for Colomer. He wasn't exactly thrifty.'

'I know absolutely nothing about it.'

'Very well. Go on.'

'I found him sitting in that chair when I got back. My manservant didn't know where I was dining, but he knew I'd be home around eleven o'clock, so he let Colomer in to wait. He was in a terrible state. Have you ever seen anyone in the grip of abject fear, Burma?'

'Yes.'

'So have I. Men about to be executed. The last morning. Well, it was rather like that with Colomer. I asked him if he was ill—'

He seemed to hesitate.

'I didn't say anything about it to the Commissaire, but I can tell you. I thought he needed the money to buy drugs.'

'Nine thousand francs for drugs!' I exclaimed. 'Who do you think he was, Cyrano de Bergerac? Anyway, it doesn't make sense. Colomer didn't use dope.'

He raised his left hand like a policeman holding up the traffic.

'I'm not a doctor. I can't judge people by their looks. But there's no need to get shirty, Burma. You remind me of Colomer. As soon as I dropped a hint about drugs he flared up and we had quite a row. I'm sorry about it now, but what's done is done. Anyhow I was angry. I gave him his money back and thought no more about him. But I'd been struck by how terrified and confused he'd seemed. Poor devil. Little did I think that two days later I'd be reading he'd been killed. And what a way to die. Obviously I was wrong about the drugs. So what's the explanation? Why did he need to run away? What was he afraid of? Some threat of revenge?'

'What for?' I said. 'Professional reasons? Political? Or something more intimate?'

Montbrison put on his charming smile.

'We can forget about crimes of passion straight away,' he said. 'As far as I know he didn't have any liaisons as dangerous as that.'

'And less dangerous ones?'

'None of those either. As for politics, I'm certain he was like me: he didn't get involved.'

'I can quite believe that. It wasn't the kind of thing he used to lose any sleep over, and I don't see why the war should have made him change his ways.'

'Professional revenge, then?'

'Commissaire Bernier tends towards that theory. He thinks Bob might have been shot by an accomplice of a bank robber Bob and I got put away. I wonder what that line of inquiry's worth.'

'Is the man he's got in mind really so dangerous?'

'He's not Little Red Riding Hood. But whether he could terrorize someone as tough as Colomer—. Frankly, Montbrison, was Colomer really in a blue funk?'

The lawyer smiled.

'Perhaps not exactly blue. Anyway, I suffer from amblyopia. But whatever it was it was real. It wasn't so bad he was crawling under the furniture. But when you saw him yourself, at the station—?'

'I didn't notice anything particular.'

'What did he say?'

'Nothing. He didn't have time. The train was pulling out. He jumped on to the running board and then collapsed.'

'Nothing to suggest he was afraid?' asked the lawyer thoughtfully, pulverizing his cigarette.

'No.'

'Then forgive me, but I come back to my first idea. Drugs. Suppose for some reason or other Colomer needs to leave Lyon in a hurry. He comes here to get his money back. I take his nervousness and anxiety to be fear, but it might have nothing to do with the journey. He might just need what I believe they call a fix. He leaves here, gets his poison, takes some, and when you meet him three hours later at the station he's as fresh as a daisy . . . What do you think of that?'

'All right. Except for one thing. I saw Colomer last at the beginning of the war. He wasn't taking drugs then. He could have changed since – I wouldn't know. But you've seen him often recently. Did he look like a drug addict?'

'I'm not a doctor', he repeated. 'Look, Burma, only the autopsy can throw any light on all this. Do you know what it showed?'

'No. Bernier hasn't breathed a word about the medical report. That can be interpreted two ways. Either there was nothing to tell. Or there was too much. Frankness and the Commissaire don't mix.'

Montbrison lit another cigarette and began to laugh.

'Did he mention Antoine Chevry or Edmond Lolhé?'

'Who might they be?'

'Friends, or rather acquaintances, of Colomer's. Oh, it's not very important. But I mentioned them in my statement.'

'He didn't say anything about them. But don't you start being secretive too. You must have been in contact with Bob enough to give me some idea about his way of life.'

'Yes. But there's not much to tell. You know better than anyone how reserved he was. Apart from myself, I don't think he saw anyone except those two young men. I introduced them to him, to help him if he started up a detective agency. That's what the money was originally intended for. But the project never got past the planning stage.'

'I see. Remind me of the names, will you?'

'Antoine Chevry and Edmond Lolhé.'

I made a note of them, then looked up inquiringly.

He shook his head.

'I don't know their addresses. Lolhé took off for Morocco, and all I've had since is a card from Marseille. Chevry got tired of living on bread and cheese and went home like a good boy to his parents, hoping they'd kill the fatted calf.

Somewhere on the Côte d'Azur. Damned if I can recall the name of the place.'

'If the name of a town or a street ever does come back to you, remember me too.'

'I will. But it's not likely to be soon, and I strongly doubt if it would help. They only met Colomer through me. So they know even less about him than I do.'

'Is Bernier having them traced?'

'I expect so. That's part of the routine, isn't it? But even if he does get hold of them they won't be able to tell him much. Cigarette? Oh, of course, you don't like them.'

'Thanks all the same. But . . . er . . . chatting away like this makes you thirsty. If I remember rightly you used to have a good cellar.'

'Crafty devil!' he cried. 'That's the question you really wanted to ask me, isn't it? You old fox! But alas! – do you think I'd have waited if I'd had anything to offer you? I've nothing left. I didn't take as many precautions for wine as I did for tobacco. Never mind. I've nothing special to do here. Let me invite you to an "ersatz" in a café. Central heating by kind permission of the customers' bodies.'

'I can't give you much time,' I said getting up. 'I've got a date with a reporter.'

'Where?'

'In a charming little café in the Passage something-or-other. I forget the name. Near the guignol theatre.'

'Would it be all right for me to come with you?'

'Perfectly all right. If you don't mind forgetting my name's Nestor Burma.'

He raised his eyebrows.

'I see!' he said. 'Very exciting. I'll come along then. We can talk about the good old days.'

Before we left, Montbrison's flunkey handed him a note that had just been delivered by a policeman on a bicycle.

He slipped it into his pocket, left the man some instructions and followed me.

Marc Covet was waiting for me in the fug of the 'Bar du Passage', silently appraising a synthetic apéritif.

'Have you got the information?' I said without preamble.

'Police after you, or something?' he replied. 'Take a seat and have whatever they've got with the most alcohol in it. No, I haven't got the information. The literary critic's gone away. His girl-friend lives on the other side of the line, and as he's got a permanent pass . . . But he'll be back tomorrow. I thought I'd better wait rather than ask someone else. If anyone has to know about my vices, I prefer it to be just the one person. Can't it wait until tomorrow?'

'Yes. It can wait.'

I finally carried out the introductions, and we sat down and had three apéritifs (a round each). Mineral water would have been dynamite in comparison.

'Let's have dinner together,' I said in disgust. 'You provide the ration tickets, I'll provide the money.'

'Done,' said Marc. 'I know a nice quiet place.'

The restaurant he took us to was full of newspaper men, some local, some from Paris. You could tell who they were by their garish clothes and the pens sticking out of their pockets. They also referred to politicians and artists by their Christian names, as if they were waiters. Some of them greeted the lawyer, but none recognized me as the director of the Fiat Lux detective agency. And I didn't hear a single mention of the murder. Marc introduced me to a few of his friends as Roly Stone. He seemed to have got attached to the name. But he was preparing the ground for the final revelation and his sensational story.

In the course of the meal I suddenly stopped chewing at my steak, which was illicit and no doubt for that reason tough. I'd had an idea.

'Marc – you said your literary critic had a permanent pass, didn't you? What about you?'

'Yes to the first question, no to the second. Pity,' he said sarcastically. 'Otherwise I presume you'd have asked me another favour. Am I right?'

'Absolutely. I have to get an urgent message to Paris. Interzone cards take for ever. If you'd been able to cross the line tonight you could have posted my letter from the first village you came to. What about you, Montbrison? No messengers amongst your contacts?'

'No,' said the lawyer. 'But I have to go to Paris myself in a few days. I've applied for a pass—'

He took out the letter that arrived just as we left his house.

'—and now I have to go to the police station about it. But that'll be too late for you.'

Marc put down his fork and took my arm.

'I can do better than that,' he said. 'You see that chap over there in the brown jacket? The one eating his dinner with his hat on? He's leaving for Paris tonight. He'll be there at seven tomorrow morning . . . Hey! Arthur!' he called. 'Come here. I want to introduce an old friend.'

The journalist with the hat finished eating and came over to our table. When the introductions had been completed – Roly Stone, Montbrison, Arthur Berger – he asked us what was on offer. Ten minutes later he'd heard and accepted his mission.

I wrote a note to Inspector Florimond Faroux, my contact at the Paris Police HQ, telling him I was having a lovely time and wished he were here, etc. I once got Faroux out of a difficult spot and he was grateful to me. In plain language my remarks about this and that conveyed that a watch on 120 rue de la Gare and a report on its inhabitants would be of great help to me. I asked him to address his reply to Marc Covet at the *Crépu*.

I let Arthur read the note.

'Not very compromising,' he chuckled.

'No. And it's addressed to a copper. That means it's sure to be safe.'

'I'll say.'

'Send it by *pneumatique*,' I suggested.

'Right. So if the train isn't derailed it'll be in your man's hands in the course of the morning. Your round, I think.'

He'd already finished his glass and drunk the remains of Marc's. We ordered a bottle of Burgundy. It was really from the Languedoc, but drinkable. We had another, and then another. We were all very merry. Although I was a bit drunk I began to feel anxious about my message. In the hands of someone like Arthur it didn't stand a chance. He'd miss his train for sure. And even if he didn't, he'd forget to post my letter. What a helpful fellow Marc was. And what an amusing bunch of mates he had!

As I was gravely ruminating, Arthur Berger was blearily boasting about his journalistic exploits, and I noticed he was staring strangely at Montbrison. He didn't take his eyes off him, glaring aggressively over the top of his glass as he drank, his head tipped forward as if above an imaginary pair of spectacles.

Suddenly he stopped dead in the middle of his ramblings to tell us confidentially that he was no ordinary bloke.

'No,' he repeated, looking at the lawyer, 'no ordinary bloke. And I'm going to prove it. How's your wound?'

'My – wound?'

Montbrison was in the same sorry state as Berger. He still wore his elegant smile, but his eyes were glazed and he was having difficulty focusing. Arthur Berger sniffed loudly, waved a shaky forefinger at him and launched into a long speech.

It appeared he had met Montbrison in June 1940 at

Combettes, a remote village where there was heavy fighting. Berger had been there as a war correspondent.

Here there was a short digression, naming the weekly concerned and indicating how stingy the editor was.

Montbrison was wounded, wasn't he? Montbrison admitted it. A slight wound on the hand? Yes. Montbrison congratulated Berger on his astonishing memory. Berger congratulated Montbrison on his decisiveness. It hadn't taken him long to dress up in civvies to avoid being taken prisoner. He, Arthur Berger, resourceful as he was, hadn't been able to do so till the next day. And so on.

I proposed a toast to their reunion. The incident had reassured me. Someone with a memory like that wouldn't forget my letter. And while we were on the subject of prisoners, or those who'd escaped being prisoners by the skin of their teeth, I told a few stories of my own.

At half past ten Arthur Berger left us. He was drunk, but still able to point himself in the right direction.

'Don't forget my letter,' I called after him.

'Next stop the cop shop!' he laughed.

Thirty minutes later, good customers though we were, the owner of the restaurant had us thrown out.

'Closing time,' he said apologetically.

Outside we nearly had a fight. The reporter and the lawyer were so overflowing with love for liberated prisoners they both wanted to put me up for the night. I said no to both, steadier in my resolve than on my feet. I wanted to go back to the hospital. This was not an acceptable excuse, as I had permission to sleep out, and if I was going back it was long past the hour for doing so.

'I'll see you home then,' Montbrison insisted.

'And so – so will I,' Marc burbled. 'The walk'll do us good.'

They left me a few yards from the building with the red cross on it.

Inside I got a dressing down from a jack-in-office who said I had no right to dress in civvies and told me if I thought I'd get permission for another outing I'd got another think coming. As I was spry enough now to climb over the wall, I just laughed in his face.

On my bed I found a letter and a suitcase. This sobered me up a bit. Both had been sent by Edouard. He was in Castelnaudary and took four pages to tell me he was in good health and hoped this found me well, and please find your things herewith.

I opened the case. Two packets of tobacco, a pair of socks and some underpants were missing. But the secret pocket I'd fixed up in the camp in case my things were searched was intact. With an unsteady hand I took out the finger prints and photograph of the prisoner who'd lost his memory. This was why I'd been so anxious to recover my luggage.

I put the two documents away safely in my shirt pocket, decanted myself into the cold sheets, lit my pipe and had the nerve to try to think.

6 Wrong address

After a while I noticed my neighbour's bed was moving. Greta Garbo emerged from underneath it and came towards me as though she wanted to speak. Then she suddenly froze and looked towards the door. The door opened and the girl in the trenchcoat came in, still holding her automatic. I leaped out of bed and took the gun away from her. Just in time, because a patient reared up out of bed number 120, which had been empty the day before. He was fully dressed and had a jeweller's attaché case in his hand. It was Eiffel Tower Joe. When I threatened him with my revolver he opened the case and took out a magnificent pearl necklace, which he put round Garbo's neck. Then I fired and he collapsed with an oath and changed into Bob Colomer. At this point a procession of reporters invaded what had now become a restaurant. I noticed Marc Covet and Arthur Berger, both obviously drunk, and was just getting ready to join them when Commissaire Bernier stopped me. Don't mix the wheat and the chaff, he told me. From now on, watertight barriers between the professions. Reporters on one side, private detectives on the other. I woke up calling myself an idiot. Out loud.

'Leave doesn't seem to agree with you,' the nurse scolded gently. 'You're all worked up. Drink this herbal tea and you'll feel better.'

I opened my eyes. The ward was full of dreary daylight. My pipe had rolled on to the floor, leaving a trail of ash across the sheet. I had a hangover. I drank the herbal tea without a murmur.

I shaved, and as the showers were working I took one. I felt much better. Then, not bothering with the office where they gave out passes, I prowled round by the kitchen quarters and was soon outside.

It was too early to do anything, so I walked along by the river and smoked a few pipes to kill time. When I heard ten o'clock strike I set to work.

First I visited a certain Monsieur Pascal, who lived in a gloomy courtyard in the rue Créqui. The 'secretary' who let me in looked more like a bodyguard. Though education is compulsory now, I suspected he couldn't read or write. He asked if I had an 'appointment'. The way he said it, together with his appearance, told me all I needed to know. I said I'd telephone, and left. M. Pascal must be a blackmailer. Not what I was looking for. I crossed him off my list.

I saw three other private detectives, so-called, who didn't please me any better. One was too smart, another not smart enough, and the third was in his second childhood. It was late afternoon when in a charming little street near the Parc de la Tête d'Or I found the man I should have started with. Needless to say he was the last on my list. His name was Gérard Lafalaise.

He was young and enthusiastic and I took to him at once. The office where he worked out his ingenious theories was clean; his secretary was pleasant and reminded me of my own Hélène Chatelain.

'My name's Nestor Burma,' I said. 'You must have read in the papers that one of my colleagues, Bob Colomer, was murdered in Perrache station the other day.'

'Of course,' he stammered.

I gave him time to get over his surprise.

'Here's what I want you to do. Colomer was thinking of setting up an agency here similar to the one in Paris. According to witnesses, he led a very secluded life. That's not surprising; he wasn't very sociable. But he might have tried to get in touch with some local detectives. I'm counting on you to find out which. I don't think he saw anyone in your agency, because you're obviously respectable' – he bowed, flattered – 'and would have told the police about it. But he certainly might have contacted some other agencies.'

'I'll do everything I can,' Lafalaise assured me. 'It's not every day you have Dynamite Burma for a client.'

'Another thing,' I said. 'You have to be a physiognomist in your job. Do you know this young lady? Do you remember ever meeting her? She's rather out of the ordinary.'

He looked up from the photograph and gave me a dubious stare.

'Very out of the ordinary,' he said drily. 'I'm afraid I don't see the joke. This is Michèle Hogan.'

'Yes. I'm looking for someone who's very like her. As I don't have a photograph of her I'm using this postcard instead. It's better than nothing. Well?'

'No,' he replied, relaxing again. 'If I had ever met anyone who looked like her I'd certainly remember.'

'How about your secretary? Or one of your detectives?'

'We can easily find out.'

He called his secretary in. During her comings and goings in town, had she ever noticed a young lady who could almost be taken for Michèle Hogan?

No, she said. The son of the woman at the dairy looked like Fernandel, but—.

'Right,' my young colleague cut in. 'If I'm not here when Paul and Victor and Prosper get back, ask them about her, please.'

After giving Lafalaise his instructions and settling his

fee, I left. Night had fallen and the fog was thicker: the
street lights, already dimmed against possible air raids,
struggled in vain to pierce it. I shivered as I crossed the
Pont de la Boucle. The nails in my boots made the metal
footway ring. You couldn't see ten feet in front of you. It
would have been child's play to push someone into the
river. On the other side of the bridge I joined a glum crowd
of passengers in a jolting, screeching tram.

The cocoon-like atmosphere of the Bar du Passage was
welcoming after my journey. I sat down near the stove.
Marc Covet arrived soon afterwards.

'The literary critic advises me to take cold showers.'

'So he's back. And the bibliography?'

'Here.' He held out a sheet of paper.

'Are these the same books as he suggested to Colomer?'

'Exactly the same.'

I folded the paper and put it with my other notes.

Marc hung his overcoat on a peg, sat down, ordered a
drink and rubbed his hands together with a shiver. Suddenly he smote himself on the forehead.

'I was forgetting I'm your letter-box,' he said. 'This came
for you. Seems to be from your friend the cop in Paris. He
didn't waste any time.'

'It helps to know the right people. But he's been remarkably quick. Could it be he's refusing to help?'

I opened Faroux's telegram. It read:

'120 rue de la Gare doesn't exist.'

7 *Le Pont de la Boucle*

That night I didn't go back to the hospital.

After a quick meal I asked Marc if he could put me up. He realized things weren't going well and made no objection. He only heaved a deeper sigh than was necessary as he stripped a couple of blankets off his bed for me.

I was just standing with one shoe still on and the broken lace in my hand when there was a knock at the door. The singsong voice of the porter informed us that Monsieur Covet was wanted on the telephone. Marc went downstairs grumbling and came back almost immediately.

'It's for you, of course,' he said. 'He's holding on.'

I looked at my watch. Midnight. Gérard Lafalaise hadn't let the grass grow under his feet.

'Hallo,' I said. 'It's me.'

'Hallo, Monsieur Burma. Lafalaise here. I must see you at once. I have some information for you.'

'Congratulations! You've been quick. Go ahead.'

'Not on the phone. It would be better for you to come here.'

'To your place? At the Tête d'Or?'

'At the Tête d'Or, yes. But not at my place. I'm not calling from my office. I'm with a friend' – he laughed – 'that I can't leave. He'd like to talk to you about film stars.'

'Marvellous! Where?'

He said it was rather complicated and he'd send someone to meet me on the Pont de la Boucle.

'How would you like a little walk in the park?' I said to Covet as I put my other shoe back on. 'Lend me a shoe-lace, would you?'

'Here you are . . . A walk? In this weather?'

'Don't forget I'm amassing material for a tiptop article.'

'What's that got to do with it?'

'Everything.'

'All right. I'll risk it. But wait while I put some heavy shoes on. I suffer from cold feet.'

'And a béret like mine to cover up your ears. Not very elegant. But we're not going courting.'

'No point in asking for an explanation, I suppose?'

I burst out laughing.

'None whatsoever.'

'Bloody awful town,' he growled when we were outside. 'I can't wait to get back to Paris.'

He moaned on about the patrols we were likely to run into, but I didn't answer so he gave up. Anyway you had to keep your mouth shut because of the fog. We went on walking in silence.

Just before we got to the bridge the shoe-lace Marc had given me let me down and I had to bend down to tie a knot in it. He went on ahead.

Apart from the swirl of the river and the clang of Marc's metal heels on the bridge, the city was strangely quiet. Everything was sunk in peaceful slumber. The reassuring rumble of a train drifted through the night. Then both the silence and the fog were pierced by a shout. It was what I'd been waiting for. I bounded forward, calling out so that Marc would know where I was, and shouting for him to do the same.

In the middle of the bridge, by the feeble yellow gold of a street lamp, I could see Covet struggling with someone who was doing his best to heave him over the parapet into the water.

When the man saw me loom up beside him he didn't panic. He felled the reporter with one terrific blow, then turned to face me. I grabbed him and we, too, fell and rolled over and over on the ground. For a moment he was on top. I was hampered by my overcoat, while he was wearing only a jacket. With a violent effort I freed myself and we were both on our feet again, like a couple of sinister dancers. The thug was obviously aiming to push me into the river now. Summoning all my strength, I loosened his grip with a tremendous punch that sent him flying back against the slippery parapet. I kneed him in the stomach and then straightened him up with an uppercut. The next thing I knew his feet were whistling past my face. I swore as I hadn't done for a long time. Then I ran over to Marc, who was getting up painfully and rubbing his chin.

'Where's the prize fighter?' he said.

'A slight error of calculation,' I replied. 'I hit him too hard . . . The railing was slippery . . . He went over.'

'You mean . . . ?'

He motioned towards the Rhône, hurtling past thirty feet beneath us.

'Yes,' I said.

'My God!'

'You can say a prayer for him some other time. For now, let's go to your office. I need to use the phone, and I don't want to have to fill in any forms first, or tell anyone my grandmother's date of birth.'

'Good idea. I need a pick-me-up and I know where there's a cupboard with some brandy in it.'

As we made our way to his office he said:

'You knew what was going to happen, of course?'

'I had a fairly good idea.'

'And you let me put on noisy boots? And had me wear a béret, so I'd look just like you?'

'Yes.'

'And made me go on in front?'

'Yes.'

'And what if I'd fallen in the drink?'

'You couldn't have. I was there, waiting for you to yell out.'

'What if you'd arrived too late? Or I hadn't had time to shout? Or you'd slipped? Or—'

'I'd still have caught the other chap. If it had been the other way round you wouldn't have known what questions to ask him. But with me on the bridge . . . '

' . . . and me floating towards Valence . . . '

'I would have avenged you.'

'You really are a nice one,' he laughed bitterly. Then after a pause he said under his breath:

'Bit late now though, even if you do know what questions to ask him.'

He seemed rather pleased about that.

'I admit it could have turned out better,' I said. 'But I hope to be able to put things right. Don't let's waste any more time.'

In the cluttered press room at the *Crépu* three reporters were playing cards in silence and clouds of smoke. They nodded to Marc and then took no more notice of us. While Covet forced the door of the cupboard, I hurried to the phone and asked for Gérard Lafalaise's office. There was no reply. That didn't surprise me.

I looked in the phone book and started calling up everyone in Lyon by the name of Lafalaise. There were plenty of them. Most were furious at being woken up, and told me to go to hell. Finally one Hector Lafalaise said he was my man's uncle. I implored him to give me his nephew's private number, and after some hestitation he agreed.

'Drink this, murderer,' said Marc, handing me a slug of brandy in a mustard glass with enough fingerprints on it to make any detective's day. I drank up and then asked the exchange for the private number. Someone said 'Hallo' in a sleepy voice. It was a servant. Monsieur Gérard wasn't in, he said.

'It's extremely important,' I bellowed. 'Where can I find him?'

I had to argue for some time, alternating persuasion and threats. Finally I got the information. Lafalaise was at a party being given by the Countess de Gasset. The servant added the aristocratic address.

'I'll be needing you again,' I said to Marc. 'This time it's high society.'

Out we went into the fog again. Covet filled me in about the countess as we went along. A birdbrain, but her behaviour seemed to be blameless. The party was being held in an elegant sixth-floor flat near Brotteaux station. A girl dressed like the maid in a musical comedy led us into a perfumed vestibule where we could hear the sound of voices, laughter and syncopated music. A door opened and Gérard Lafalaise came towards us, his hand outstretched. There was a look of genuine astonishment on his face.

'Well!' he exclaimed. 'This *is* a surprise. You were the last person I expected to see here tonight.'

'Our job's full of surprises,' I said. 'And this is certainly the night for them. I've just had one myself, on the Pont de la Boucle. One of my admirers tried to chuck me off it.'

'What!' He was speechless.

'Let's find a quiet corner,' I said.

We did so and I told him what had happened.

'The man on the phone didn't know that you and I had agreed to use Christian names,' I said, 'so when he called me "Monsieur Burma" I was on to him at once.'

'What happened to him?'

'Well, he won't die from heatstroke this summer, that's for sure. He's in the fridge. Now I suggest you put your coat on and come with me.'

'Where to?'

'No idea. You're the one with the address. I want to go and see your charming secretary . . . I don't even know her name.'

'Louise Brel. But I don't understand.'

'She seemed too stupid to be true this afternoon. Don't you remember, when you asked her about Michèle Hogan and she started talking about Fernandel? She'd have babbled anything to cover her confusion. She knows the girl I'm looking for, and for some reason my activity's bothering her. So tonight she tried to put an end to it before I got any further. She had easy access to your notes, so she knew where to contact me. Then she sent a killer to do the necessary.'

He shook his head disbelievingly.

'It's incredible. Look, I'm only a provincial detective and I know it may seem impertinent, saying this to Dynamite Burma . . . But are you sure you're not mistaken? Was it really Louise who telephoned you?'

'No. She left everything to the chap. Even the dive into the river. Although that wasn't really planned.'

'I can't believe it,' he murmured. Then more forcefully: 'You must be mistaken.'

'The best way to make sure is to go and see the girl,' I said impatiently. 'If you stand there all night telling me how you trust her, she'll have hopped it by the time we get there. Are you ready?'

'Yes. But it's incredible,' he repeated. 'A glass of rum before we go?'

'No. Half a bottle.'

8 Louise Brel

Dishevelled though she was, Mlle. Louise Brel looked charming. She'd thrown on an opal négligée that suited her down to the ground, where her bare feet with their varnished toe-nails nestled in a luxurious bedside rug. Quite a picture. But it was no thanks to her I was still around to look at it.

When Lafalaise rang the bell at the stylish little suburban villa and called out his name, she'd suppressed an exclamation of surprise. Then, after a good deal of fuss she opened the door to let us in. When she saw the three of us standing there she almost shut it again. I don't blame her. I was wearing my most intimidating expression.

But now we were standing in her tiny, spotless, cosily feminine bedroom. She seemed not to understand what was going on. Her eyes were puffy with sleep and she looked inquiringly from one to the other of us. But her bosom rose and fell anxiously under her silk wrap.

I stuck my hand into my overcoat pocket and held my pipe like a pistol.

'Put some clothes on,' I ordered. 'Get your identity papers and come with us. Commissaire Bernier would like you to answer some questions about an attack one of your accomplices made on me a little while ago.'

She stared at me, dumbfounded. Then she turned to her

boss for help. He was obviously embarrassed and darted pitying looks at her that I wasn't meant to see.

'I've tried to tell M. Burma he's mistaken,' he said protectively. 'I simply can't believe you're a criminal. But he says you set a trap for him. It's . . . It's . . . Well, don't just stand there, Louise. Say something! Defend yourself!'

'What for? Against whom?' she said. 'I don't understand what I'm supposed to have done. I never set any trap—'

'Do you know this girl?' I held the film star's photograph under her nose.

'Yes. It's Michèle Hogan.'

'Thank you,' I said sarcastically. 'I didn't realize. But do you know anyone who looks like her? Careful, we've already asked you this question before. This afternoon.'

'I remember.'

'You still haven't answered me. Do you know anyone who looks like Michèle Hogan?'

'No.'

I brought my face up close to hers.

'Do you know anyone who looks like Michèle Hogan?'

'No.'

I grabbed her wrists and squeezed them hard.

'You're lying!'

'No, I'm not,' she said. 'Let go! You're hurting me.'

She tried to pull away, knocked against the bed and sat down heavily.

'Now it's my turn to say no. I'll let you go when you're more cooperative, my beauty. Now. Do you know—'

I was interrupted by Gérard Lafalaise. He put his hand on my arm and glared straight into my eyes. It was the first time I'd seen him show any kind of aggression.

'Monsieur Burma,' he hissed reproachfully. 'This game has gone on long enough. I should never have gone along with your outrageous suspicions. Perhaps I was influenced by your reputation. Anyhow I won't be a party to it any longer. I wish I'd never brought you here. Kindly stop molesting this young lady at once. I can guarantee her innocence. These methods are not worthy of you, and—'

'Shut up,' I said. 'Someone tried to throw me in the river. That's all that matters as far as I'm concerned. But I am prepared to free this little angel's wrists just long enough to show you why I'm called Dynamite Burma.'

My fist shot out and caught him squarely on the chin, dropping him to the floor just next to his hat. I threw a scarf to Covet.

'Tie him up', I said. 'This room isn't big enough for to let him wave his arms about. And pop a cork in him. He might want to sing when he wakes up, and I don't much care for his repertoire.'

'See you in gaol, Nestor,' Covet groaned. But he did as I said.

Everything had happened so quickly, Louise Brel hadn't had time to try to escape. She was still sitting on the rumpled bed, apparently in a dream. When I went up to her she shoved me away and said that if we didn't clear off she'd scream for the police. That tickled me.

'The police?' I said. 'Didn't I invite you to come to the station right at the start? Commissaire Bernier would be delighted to see you. I'm not afraid of the police, my love.'

This wasn't true. If a copper arrived I'd be in a fix.

'If anyone should be, it's you. You claim not to know this girl. Yet you sent me off to a bogus appointment this evening, a trap, all to prevent me from finding out any more about her. I want to know why. The trap was set over the phone. Well, only one person in Lyon knew my number: your boss. And only one other person had access to that information: his secretary. I didn't suspect him because he answered my questions frankly this afternoon. But you didn't. You tried to cover your confusion by telling some idiotic story that didn't tie in with the expression on your face.

You don't look stupid, if you'll allow the compliment. So when this fellow tried to help me explore the depths of the Rhône, it didn't take me long to work it out.'

I took out my pipe, then my pouch, and put them both back in my pocket with a groan. The pouch was empty.

'Well?' I went on. 'Still want to call the police? Coppers in uniform aren't very bright. Better try a Commissaire. Bernier, for example. The one in charge of the inquiry into Colomer's death.'

I watched her closely as I said this. I was wasting my time. She stared at me with growing astonishment. Then she said suddenly:

'So that's it.'

Her voice had changed. She put her head in her hands, lay down on the bed and began to cry softly.

'If you're just trying to gain time it won't work,' I said harshly.

She sniffed.

'Did they really try to throw you into the river?'

'I suppose you didn't know about it.'

'No. I didn't.'

'Of course not. Any more than you know a girl who looks like Michèle Hogan.'

'But I do know that.'

'At last. Name? Address?'

'I don't know.'

'Here we go again.'

'It's the truth. Why won't you believe me? Oh, I understand how you must feel – if you were almost thrown into the river—'

'Thanks to you.'

'Yes, because of me. But I'm not guilty.'

'If we add up all these half-confessions we'll finally get to the truth. Take your time. I'm in no hurry. What's the link between you and this girl? Why—'

'Please. Don't ask any more questions.'

Then, with a weary gesture: 'I'll tell you everything.'

'Right. Try to lie with moderation.'

'I won't lie.' She sniffed, took out a handkerchief, blew her nose and dried her eyes.

'I knew her because I'd seen her several times with Paul. She's very beautiful. I thought they were lovers.'

'Who's Paul?'

'Paul Carhaix. He works at the agency.'

'Does he now? What does he look like?'

The description she gave fitted my attacker, though what with the darkness and the briefness of the struggle I hadn't really got a good look at him.

'When you asked me if I knew someone who looked like Michèle Hogan this afternoon, I realized it must be important. I knew you were the famous Nestor Burma. So I thought Paul's friend might be in danger. I decided not to say anything before I'd told him about it. So I said I didn't know her. But I'm a hopeless liar. I was sure I'd given myself away. And so I had.'

She looked at me almost admiringly.

'There's no doubt about it – you don't miss much.'

'Oh, well,' I said gaily. 'My name is Burma. The man who can KO any mystery.'

'Talking of knock-outs,' Covet remarked, 'your victim's coming round.'

It was true: the heap in the corner was moving.

'Take his gag out,' I said.

'You can untie me as well,' Lafalaise groaned. 'You're right. I'm awake and I've heard every word of Mademoiselle Brel's confession. I admit I was wrong to doubt you, Burma. You've had more experience than I have, and your judgement is better. I apologize. Rushing to interfere like that, I almost—'

'Want me to stick your gag back in again? Still, while we're all apologizing, I'm sorry I had to put you on your back. I didn't have much choice. Now sit down in the corner and keep quiet. Mademoiselle Brel hasn't finished the story of Snow White and the Big Bad Wolf yet.'

I turned back to her. 'Go on,' I said encouragingly.

'Would you mind switching the electric fire on, please?' she said. She was shivering under her flimsy nightdress. The newspaperman-of-all-work had been rubbing his hands together to keep them warm for the last few minutes, and didn't have to be asked twice.

'When Paul got back to the office this evening, after Monsieur Lafalaise had left,' Mademoiselle Brel went on, 'I told him trouble was brewing for his friend. She seemed so sweet I couldn't believe she'd do anything wrong. And Paul has always struck me as perfectly respectable. But from what you say it seems I'll have to revise my opinion.'

'I'm afraid so. But let's keep to the point. What exactly did you tell him?'

'That Nestor Burma had been to see the boss, and they both seemed to be looking for the girl. I said I thought it was some terrible mistake, and someone must have been plotting against her. He thanked me for not saying anything. He seemed really grateful, and said of course she was above suspicion and he personally was going to ask Nestor Burma for an explanation. He wanted your address. I was in too deep to say no. I said you'd left a telephone number. He told me he wouldn't breathe a word about it, and I gave it to him. I didn't think I was doing anything wrong. I never imagined the consequences could be so . . . tragic. And now . . . '

'Don't worry', I said. 'I'm not dead. What's her name?'

'I don't know.'

'Sure?'

'Quite sure, Monsieur Burma.'

'During the conversation you had with Carhaix about her, didn't he let anything slip out? Not even her Christian name?'

'No. Not even her Christian name.'

'And when you met them before? Didn't he introduce you?'

'No. I only passed them on the other side of the street.'

'Oh. And you're sure he didn't mention her name this evening?'

'Absolutely sure.'

'Are they lovers?'

'I . . . I think so.'

'Not certain?'

'No.'

'Thank you.'

I turned to her employer.

'So, Monsieur Lafalaise, do you see? Your employee Paul Carhaix had good reason to try to stop me investigating his protégée – they're not lovers or he'd certainly have let her name out in the heat of the discussion. She's probably just an acquaintance, or someone who's employing him behind your back. So, once he's got the number out of Mademoiselle Brel he phones me, imitating your voice, and tells me he's with someone who can give me some information about the girl I'm looking for. Then he fixes to meet me in a place that's difficult for anyone but a local to find, and says he'll send someone to meet me "just to make sure". Quite a humorist. And then he attacks me on the Pont de la Boucle.'

'What happened to him?' asked Louise Brel.

'Do you love him?' I asked.

'We used to be lovers. He stopped loving me, but I still love him. That's why I didn't want to admit my rival was the person you were looking for. That's why I warned him.

I didn't want him to suffer, even indirectly. What has happened to him?'

'Try to forget him', I said. 'You won't see him again. He ran away. He wasn't worthy of you.'

9 The search

We went back to the car. Gérard Lafalaise was one of the lucky few who had a permit. Just as well with all those comings and goings.

'Let's go to this Paul's place,' I said. 'I was wrong about your secretary. It makes me regret all the more that I can't bring him back to life. But maybe if we search his hideout I'll get a brilliant idea.'

'Are you – are you going to tell the police?' Lafalaise asked timidly. He knew something about my methods now, as well as my intuition.

'All in good time. We'll have to agree on the same story first. I can't have you saying more than I think fit to say myself.'

'Of course,' he said, delighted to be my accomplice and thus emboldened to ask, after a moment's silence:

'Why are you looking for this girl who's so like Michèle Hogan?'

'I met her on a bus one evening and I've had a crush on her ever since.'

Marc took the cigarette out of his mouth to give vent to his hilarity.

'Well?' he said to Lafalaise. 'Satisfied? Remember what he said about the police a minute ago? The day you hear Burma pouring his heart out, send me a wire – we'll bring out a special edition. He told me she was his daughter, and was stolen by the gypsies the day of her first communion.'

'That wasn't true either,' I said smiling.

At that moment we were held up by a patrol.

Lafalaise produced a special pass which must have been issued by some bigwig, because the policeman just saluted and let us go, merely pointing out respectfully that our headlamps were a little too bright. They weren't terribly strict about air-raid precautions here in the unoccupied zone, he said, and the black-out wasn't rigorously enforced, but some unidentified aircraft had flown over the week before so it was best to be careful. Lafalaise drove off, disregarding this observation, and I thanked my stars I'd chosen to work with someone with so much pull.

Half-past three was striking in the distance as we arrived at the dead man's domicile. It was a two-room flat on the second floor and looked out on the street. There was no concierge, but the gate into the courtyard was open. Lucky again. To get into the flat itself I called on Marc Covet's special talents. If you gave him a hairpin he could get you into the vaults of the Bank of France.

'After you,' he said, standing aside.

As soon as we switched the lights on we realized Monsieur Paul Carhaix was a man who liked to see things clearly. None of the bulbs was less than 150 watts.

'I advise you to keep your gloves on,' I warned my companions. 'The police will give the place a going over sooner or later. No point in leaving them too many fingerprints.'

They complied with my suggestion, and we started to search the flat with a fine tooth comb.

'Are we looking for anything in particular?' asked Lafalaise.

'The name of a woman, and if possible her address.'

We inspected all the drawers, a writing pad, some envelopes and a few chaotic shelves of cheap books. A board on a trestle did duty as a desk. On it stood a pot of ink, a pen, and a give-away ashtray. We searched them all without success. M. Paul Carhaix was evidently an orderly chap who didn't leave things lying about.

'I'd swear this place has been cleaned up recently,' said Covet.

'Yes. He probably didn't intend to come back after he'd got rid of me. But is that rational behaviour?'

'No, obviously not. But a criminal and a madman are one and the same thing.'

I opened the wardrobe. Inside were two hats, three pairs of trousers, a jacket, two overcoats and a raincoat.

'How many overcoats did Carhaix own?' I asked Lafalaise.

'I only ever saw two,' he said. 'A dark grey one and . . . Well, I'm damned – both of them are there.'

'He was only wearing a jacket when he attacked me, so as to be able to move more easily. But I presume if he'd intended to disappear after the murder he'd have taken at least one overcoat with him and put it down somewhere before the fight. But we didn't see one anywhere, even though it's not the time of year when you can afford to be without one. And buying a new one isn't too easy – I'm only just back from prisoner of war camp myself, but I seem to have heard something about clothes rationing.'

'Our genius seems to be completely at sea,' said Marc, 'so allow my feeble intelligence to throw some light on the proceedings. Your attacker tidied up everything here and got rid of all compromising documents – if there were any – before he set his trap. If it worked he intended to vanish into the blue. But there was nothing to stop him coming back here first, changing into some decent clothes, picking up his suitcase, and then disappearing.'

'Quite true,' agreed Lafalaise.

'It's possible,' I said.

There was a suitcase in the bottom of the wardrobe. It obviously hadn't been packed ready to be picked up, but I made no comment. We searched it, as we did the pockets of all the clothes. Not so much as a tram ticket.

'All right, let's go,' I said. I was neither altogether satisfied nor altogether disappointed. 'No point in hanging about.'

Just at that moment Marc gave a shout of triumph. At the bottom of the kitchen cupboard, under a pile of old newspapers, were dozens of empty bottles that had once contained lighter fuel, and a pair of shoes. In one of the shoes he'd found a revolver.

I took hold of it carefully. It was a .32 automatic of foreign make. The shape of the barrel was unusual, and I couldn't tell if it had been used recently. Covet showed me exactly where he'd found it. Not the best hiding place in the world.

I said it wasn't a very interesting discovery and told him to put it back. Then I led the way out.

Gérard Lafalaise drove us back to Marc's hotel. Before he left us I made him repeat his version of events, so that it wouldn't differ from what I'd decided to tell Bernier. I made him promise to say nothing about his comings and goings with us during the night, and to impress upon Louise Brel that she must keep quiet too.

'Charming evening,' said Marc, as he got undresed. 'Assault and battery, which nearly put paid to me. A body in the river. Third degree of attractive blonde. KO, gagging and binding of a professional colleague. Breaking and entering of dead murderer's premises, and searching of same without a warrant. You certainly make things hum.'

My pipe had gone out. I chewed on the stem while he went on with his monologue.

'To make myself useful I dig up the key to the whole

case. Here's a clue, surely! But no – we're underestimating the famous Nestor Burma. "Put that toy back where you found it," says the genius. "It's of no importance."'

But he had to admit that we can't all have the knack.

'You really shook up Louise what's-her-name, though,' he went on. 'She's not bad looking. Very pretty eyes. Unfortunately she's as suited to working for a detective agency as you are to running a temperance society. She allows her emotions to run away with her, and casts suspicion on her own Sherlock Holmes. Hélène Chatelain wouldn't do a thing like that.'

'How do you know?'

'Good God! Found your tongue again? Don't tell me my conversation interests you!'

'Detectives' secretaries are all the same.'

'How can you say a thing like that?'

He looked at me solicitously.

'Something the matter? Oh, I see. You're out of tobacco.'

He pointed at his jacket, lying on the chair where he'd thrown it.

'Have a cigarette.'

'No. I only like a pipe.'

'Dismantle a Gauloise, then, and stick that in.'

'No.'

'A drop of rum, then? I think I've—'

'Just leave me alone and go on asking questions and giving yourself the answers.'

'Probably the best thing to do with you in that mood,' he sighed. 'Anyway, it's five o'clock. You should get some rest.'

'No. If you don't mind, I'm going to think for a bit. Then I'll go out for a breath of fresh air.'

'Whatever you like, so long as you stop pacing up and down like that. You're making me seasick.'

10 Rue de Lyon

Before going to give my version of events to the Commissaire, I wanted to have a chat with Julien Montbrison. He hadn't got his reputation for nothing. He was a brilliant lawyer and his advice might be useful. At seven o'clock I rang the front-door bell in the rue Alfred-Jarry.

The manservant looked seedier than ever and made a lot of fuss about letting me in. The master was still in bed. This was hardly a suitable hour. Etc. But he finally agreed to tell Maître Montbrison I was there.

As I expected, he came back and let me in. He asked me to wait in the study, and to kill time I looked at a copy I found there of Poe's short stories, with Dominguez's illustrations. Then I played with the contents of an ashtray. By the time the portly lawyer joined me I was reduced to twiddling my thumbs.

He'd run a comb through his hair and put on an expensive dressing gown, and kept his hands in his pockets as if he was cold. He looked rather bewildered, as anyone might who'd just been rudely awakened. His outstretched hand glittered. Obviously he wore the famous rings even in bed.

'To what do I owe the pleasure of this early visit?' he said with a hint of reproach, eyeing the clock.

'I'm sorry to get you out of bed,' I said, 'but I need your advice. I'm going to see Commissaire Bernier in half an hour, and in the course of the conversation I'm going to admit to tipping a man into the river last night.'

Montbrison started, and dropped the cigarette he must have lit as soon as he got out of bed.

'Nothing surprises me coming from Nestor Burma. But all the same! . . . What happened?'

I told him I'd employed a detective to find out what Colomer had been up to in Lyon. As far as that was possible, of course. And that this idiot seemed to have gone and shot his mouth off. And one of the murderer's accomplices, or the murderer himself, must have heard about it and laid an ambush for me. But I was less decrepit than I looked and had managed to break free. So the thug had taken a dive into the river instead of me.

'Splendid,' he said with a wan smile. 'Your story's woken me up better than any ersatz coffee. First, congratulations on escaping with your life. Next, what can I do for you?'

'Give me a few professional tips. I'm wondering how Bernier's going to take all this. He knows me, of course, but only by reputation. And private detectives' reputations—'

'Quite. But . . . do you really have to put him in the picture?'

'It's unavoidable. This is all linked to Bob's death, and I want his death avenged.'

'If your attacker and the one at the station are both the same person there's not much to be done. The fishes will be the jury! And the sentence has been carried out before it was pronounced.'

'Maybe. But my mind's made up. And if Bernier got difficult . . . I don't know – say he had doubts about legitimate self-defence. If there *were* any difficulties, could you smooth them over?'

'But of course.'

He lit another cigarette and we drew up a plan of campaign. I hoped I wouldn't have to use it.

I pushed back my chair.

'Would you like me to come with you?' he asked.

'Are you mad? What would they think if they saw me arriving with my lawyer? They'd slap the handcuffs on me right away!'

He laughed and didn't insist. I promised to keep him informed and left.

I still had plenty of time to spare. I wrote three interzone cards in a nearby post office, then bought some bread and went into a bar, where I washed the bread down with some over-saccharined coffee. Then I bought myself a packet of shag and filled my pipe as I made my way to the police station. Bernier didn't hide his astonishment at seeing me so early.

'Got the killer hidden under your coat?' he said. 'Good Lord, what have you been up to? You've got eyes like a Russian rabbit!'

There were bags under his, but I politely refrained from drawing attention to them.

'I've been out on the spree with my nurse,' I said. 'You should see her! I prefer Russian rabbits' eyes to dead fishes' eyes any day.'

'I'm sure. Is that all you've come to tell me?'

'Yes. I've been thinking it up all night. Amusing, isn't it?'

'Hilarious. Come on, spit it out. Don't keep me in suspense.'

'I was crossing the Pont de la Boucle last night when someone grabbed me with the obvious intention of trying to push me into the river. He was tough, but not as tough as me, even though I am an ex-POW. We had an animated discussion, then he swam off. I think he must be training for the Olympic Games.'

The veins on the Commissaire's nose turned a rich claret colour. His jaw dropped and he pounded on his desk until everything on it jumped up and down. Each thump was accompanied by an oath. After he'd calmed down again I went on with my yarn. He listened in silence, and although he changed colour again once or twice he didn't seem to doubt a word of it. Things were going better than I'd hoped.

'That'll teach you to use private detectives!' he scoffed when I'd finished. 'They're all—' He stopped dead.

'Don't forget I'm one,' I said quietly.

'I just remembered.'

He asked for more details, which I willingly supplied. That's to say, I left out a lot. He didn't need to know about Mlle Brel's sentimental attachments, nor about our nocturnal visit to Paul Carhaix's flat.

Commissaire Bernier frowned.

'This detective,' he said. 'Lafalaise. Is he trustworthy? He couldn't have done it, could he?'

'I saw him a little while ago. He didn't look as if he'd just climbed out of the river.'

'That's not what I meant. He could have been behind it.'

'You're barking up the wrong tree there, Commissaire,' I said firmly. 'He's just a fool with a loose tongue, though he won't admit it. He was so proud to have me as a client, he lost his head.'

'Hm . . . Still, we must leave nothing to chance. I'll have him watched.'

He seized the telephone and spent the next quarter of an hour shouting orders all over the building. The river and hotel police received his particular attention. When he put the phone down he was streaming with perspiration.

'Tonight – tomorrow at the latest – we'll have your man,' he said. 'We'll drag the river if we have to. He can't have got far. What a fool, attacking you like that. He, or who-ever's behind him, must have been afraid you'd find out the truth. Oh, well, it's just another case taking the usual course. We're in the dark for days, then suddenly someone does something silly and the problem's solved.'

He'd still be counting his chickens now if I hadn't interrupted.

'What does the autopsy say?' I asked.

He laughed. 'Wait till we've fished him up first.'

'I'm talking about the Colomer case.'

He was serious again.

'Didn't I show it to you? Nothing particular. Automatic pistol. Six .32 bullets in the back . . . By the way—'

'Yes?'

'Was the man who attacked you French?'

'And did his grandmother ride a bicycle? Sorry, I forgot to ask.'

'You might have noticed. There's usually some shouting and yelling when there's a fight. You didn't notice any accent?'

'No. Why?'

'Nothing.'

He launched into a diatribe against foreigners. I interrupted again.

'No idea where the bank notes Colomer was carrying came from?'

'No. Montbrison doesn't know either. Why? Are you bothered by the amount?'

'Yes. Nine thousand francs – Bob could never have saved that much.'

'My dear Burma,' said the Commissaire patronizingly, 'we're living in curious times. I know people in Lyon who were paupers once and who are princes today.'

'What's the recipe?'

'Black market. What do you say to that?'

'Nothing.'

I got up. I told the Commissaire where he could reach me if he had any news, agreed to keep an evening free soon for a game of his favourite poker, and left.

I was soon climbing the chilly marble staircase of the nearby library, and unfolding the list Marc had given me as I entered the silent reading room. A grim-looking assistant brought me the volumes I asked for. I hit on the right one first time: *The Origins of the Gothic Novel in France*, by Maurice Ache. It fell open at the page where the last reader had left a slip of paper. My heart leapt as I recognized what looked like Colomer's writing.

'Coming from Lyon,' I read, 'and after meeting the divine and infernal marquis, this is the most prodijious of all his works.'

Bob had inherited his parents' bad spelling. But now that helped to clinch my certainty that the writing was his.

He had consulted the books about Sade in hopes of finding the solution to the riddle. He found the answer he sought, and in his excitement had left it behind.

But he *had* found it.

There was a nail-mark in the margin beside one sentence. I could just see Colomer gleefully making it.

'Unparalleled in any other literature, and preceding Ann Radcliffe's first novel by four years and Lewis' famous *Monk* by eleven, this prodigious work . . . '

The reference was to *The 120 Days of Sodom*. 120 . . . a street number.

In which street? The rue de la Gare?

No, not the rue de la Gare. Florimond Faroux's telegram had been categorical. '120 rue de la Gare doesn't exist.' So?

I went back to the cryptogram.

'Coming from Lyon . . . ' The words 'gare' and 'Lyon' danced about in my head. My subconscious associated the two, and suddenly I found myself wondering whether what we were looking for was not the rue de la Gare but the rue de (la gare de) Lyon.

So, setting aside the mystery of why two people on the point of death should have uttered a secret formula instead of giving some definite information, I was beginning to see a glimmering of sense.

I knew someone who lived in the rue de Lyon. Someone I'd been meaning to look up since I got back. But the house in question was number 60, not number 120. Half of 120 . . . What a coincidence. The divine and infernal Marquis . . . In a simplistic interpretation: half good, half bad. Half and half.

The reasoning wasn't as crazy as it might seem at first sight. I'd had a vague feeling I ought to find a place for Hélène Chatelain, my ex-secretary, in this puzzle. I'd asked Marc a few questions about her activities, and rightly or wrongly I believed she was mixed up in Colomer's death, or at least in the mystery leading up to it.

I couldn't forget that one of the two men who had used their last breath to pronounce the mysterious address had preceded it by the name Hélène.

Of course my ex-secretary wasn't the only woman called Hélène, and after No. 60202's death it hadn't even crossed my mind that she might know him. But since then Colomer had been killed. And he knew both Hélène and the phrase '120 rue de la Gare'. Strange coincidences, to say the least. Hence my equation: 120 rue de la Gare = 60 rue de Lyon. Not entirely without foundation, nor yet very subtle, but it was the most economical theory, and the one that tied in best with my growing suspicions.

All these ideas had shaken me up a bit. I abandoned the Marquis de Sade, put Colomer's note in my pocket, and went to a café. There I wrote another letter to Florimond Faroux, which I sent that afternoon by one of the useful newspapermen who kept flitting back and forth between the occupied and unoccupied zones. Like my previous message, it was in code. When deciphered it said:

'Telegram received. Thanks. Have Hélène Chatelain my ex-secretary followed. Address 60 rue de Lyon.'

11 The killer

Towards midday I dropped in at the hospital. No one seemed to have noticed my absence. I met the nurse in the courtyard. Surely she must have realized. But she just said hallo. And I walked out again as easily as I'd walked in. The fog of the last few days had given way to a pale sun. I strolled down to the river.

The river police were searching the bed of the Rhône. A small crowd stood gaping. The searchers didn't seem to be having any luck. Some way off, in a little boat, I spotted a raincoat and a grey trilby. They belonged to a red-faced man who was barking out furious orders. I weighed up what line I should take and went down on to the quay.

I was just about to be rash and call out to the Commissaire when a policeman in uniform jumped into a boat and began to row towards the flagship. I couldn't catch what he said to Bernier, but both boats soon left the middle of the river and came over to the bank near where I was standing.

'Oh, there you are,' said Bernier, recognizing me. 'Perfect timing. I've just been told they've pulled someone out up at La Mulatière, a bit further down the river. He wasn't wearing an overcoat, but he's not a tramp. It must be your man. Come and identify him.'

He gave some instructions, ordered the whole fleet back to port and then we jumped into the police car. Another car followed behind with the forensic experts, photographers, doctors and the rest, and we all sped away along by the river.

On the way the Commissaire told me he'd abandoned the theory that Colomer had been killed by gangsters with whom he'd been dabbling in the black market.

'Yes, you mentioned it before,' I said. 'What made you think that?'

'The nine thousand francs. You'd said Colomer lived from hand to mouth. But this morning, just after you left, a very distinguished citizen of Lyon told me Colomer had been working for her on a very delicate matter. He conducted the inquiry brilliantly, and charged a lot because he needed the money to set up an agency. So that's where the cash came from.'

We were met by the taciturn policeman who was with Bernier when he visited me in hospital. He'd become chattier since.

'Stiff's at the station,' he said.

The corpse was laid out on a plank. He was a well-built young man, dressed in what must once have been a good suit. His hair was plastered to his forehead and his face bore all the marks of death by drowning.

While the Commissaire's men were photographing him from every angle and taking his fingerprints, Bernier asked me if I recognized him.

'He's changed a bit since yesterday,' I said. 'But it's definitely him.'

'Had you seen him before?'

'Not till he started to take an interest in me.'

The photographer told us he'd finished and the doctor began a brief examination. We watched in silence. The Commissaire's cigarette had gone out, but he kept the butt in the corner of his mouth. I smoked one pipe after another.

Finally the doctor straightened up and told us cause of death, length of time in water, etc. Nothing out of the way.

'Heavy bruising on the chin,' he said. 'A masterly punch.'

The Commissaire turned to me.

'Your handiwork, no doubt?'

'No doubt,' I replied.

The doctor looked me up and down and blinked. But he didn't say anything. He shut his bag and left.

'Now let's have our friend searched,' the Commissaire ordered.

One of his men came reluctantly forward. No sooner had he touched the corpse's clothes than he started to complain.

'Ugh. They're freezing,' he said. Very original. From the pockets he slowly extracted a packet of cigarettes, a handkerchief, a pair of gloves, a wallet, a purse, a pencil, a pen, a watch, a lighter, a tube of flints and a bunch of keys. Everything that wasn't metal was of course in a sorry state. Bernier grabbed the wallet. It contained army papers in the name of Paul Carhaix, some medical brochures of a certian kind, a rent receipt, four one-hundred franc notes and . . .

'Perhaps it wasn't a complete waste of time having your Lafalaise followed,' he said. 'Look who this chap was working for.' He brandished Carhaix's business card.

'Not surprising he was so well informed,' I said.

'Especially if it was his boss who tipped him the wink.'

I shook my head.

'I'd be very surprised,' I said.

He shrugged.

'Be that as it may,' he chuckled, 'we've been getting throught a hell of a lot of private detectives over the last few days. I'd keep my eyes skinned if I were you.'

'I am,' I replied. 'That's why it's him lying there and not me.'

He took down the address on the receipt.

'Let's go and have a look where he lived,' he said. 'One of these keys must open the door. You can come along if you like.'

I didn't like, but it would have looked suspicious if I'd refused. So I squeezed in between the two inspectors already waiting in the car, and we set off.

I quailed a bit when the policeman inserted the key in the lock. Would he notice it had been picked? But Marc had done a good job. Then it struck me that it didn't matter anyway.

The flat was just as we'd left it. I pretended to be very interested in the search, laughing up my sleeve all the time. They didn't find anything of interest, and Bernier's good humour was just beginning to evaporate when he noticed something I'd missed the night before.

'You'd think he was a commercial traveller,' he said. He lifted the suitcase out of the wardrobe and took out an impressive array of gloves, which he spread out on the floor.

'Winter gloves, summer gloves,' he grunted. 'Gloves for every season of the year. It makes you think—'

'He was certainly a prudent fellow,' I said. 'Did you notice how few things he had in his wallet? Just the minimum. Not a single item that was unnecessary."

'Or compromising.'

'And this flat in apple-pie order.'

'Yes. But even the most careful criminal can forget something which leads him straight to the scaffold.'

'You wouldn't guillotine a corpse?'

'Just a figure of speech.'

At that moment, doubtless to confirm the Commissaire's theory, the policeman poking about in the kitchen let out an exclamation. He was gingerly holding up the revolver which he'd just found in an old shoe.

'Well,' Bernier trumpeted. 'What did I tell you?'

He bent over the weapon, devouring it with his eyes but not touching it, then sniffing at it like a dog hesitating over a doubtful bone. His complexion had gone several shades pinker with excitement.

'Foreign,' he said. 'Automatic. Fitted with a silencer. Looks like a .32.'

'Does that suggest anything to you?' I said.

'The same as it does to you.'

I denied having any ideas at all, but no one was listening. Finally the Commissaire wrapped the gun up carefully in a handkerchief and put it away in a box. Then they continued their search. I was itching to tell them they wouldn't find anything else, but as I couldn't very well do that I waited patiently until they'd convinced themselves that the pistol was the only discovery they'd make. Then we went back to the car.

The Inspector held out his hand before he got in, indicating that he'd seen enough of me.

'Thank you for identifying your – er – victim. I'm afraid I've got a lot of things to do now. I can't let you in on every step of my investigation. Leave me a phone number so that I can reach you if I need you.'

'All right,' I said, 'but don't leave me here – I'll never get a taxi. Drop me at the Place Bellecour. It's on your way.'

Ten minutes later I was in the Bar du Passage. I might have been thrown out for not paying in my youth but they'd have to admit I was making up for it now. The place was virtually empty. I sat down in a corner and ordered a beer.

The usual contingent of regulars came in before dinner, Marc Covet among them. I filled him in on the latest developments, then we talked about life in general and went and had a meal. After that, back we went to the Bar du Passage. At ten o'clock the phone rang and woke up the waiter. When he came over to our table he looked just as dusty but less nonchalant than usual. He was obviously shaken.

'Which of you is Monsieur Nestor Burma?' he croaked. 'It's a pol . . . a Comm . . . ' He couldn't get the words out, so I left him to it. Marc showed me where the phone was and I picked it up so hastily I nearly flattened my ear.

'Hallo! Nestor Burma here.'

'It's Commissaire Bernier,' said a jubilant voice. 'I don't know what you've been doing since we parted, but I haven't been wasting time. The mystery's solved. The i's are dotted and the t's are crossed. Or almost. Would you like to come over? The stove's red hot and I've got some imitation coffee to put on it. I'm in the mood for a chat.'

'I'm on my way,' I said.

In his gloomy little office on the Quai de Saône, Commissaire Bernier was waiting for me behind a curtain of grey smoke. He might have been in ambush. The stove glowed red in one corner of the room. On it stood a saucepan. A strange aroma filled the air. It really was imitation coffee.

Outside it was getting colder. No fog, but a nasty penetrating drizzle. This town was getting more and more hospitable.

'Sit down,' he said jovially. 'The case is almost over. We'll soon be able to have that game of poker we talked about. In the meantime we're going to sit and look at some pictures like a couple of good little boys. I've earned a bit of relaxation.'

He poured the coffee, put in generous amounts of real sugar, lit a cigarette and added two more clouds of smoke to the fug, then opened a drawer and took out a revolver with a label on it. It was the weapon from Carhaix's flat, still flecked with white lead dust from the fingerprinting.

'Don't be afraid to handle it,' said Bernier. 'It was as clean as a whistle. Not a single print on it. Obviously been wiped before it was put away. Careful fellow, that! All we found were some glove marks – his, no doubt. But they're of no interest at this stage. What do you make of the gun?'

'What do you make of it?'

'It's an automatic. Foreign. A .32, as I thought. The bullets fired by it are identical to the ones your friend was killed with. And here are a few instructive photos. These are the bullets taken from Colomer's body. They've been rolled on a sheet of tin so that any grooves on the surface are printed on to the sheet. And here's the result of the same process applied to bullets fired in the lab from the gun we've got here – the one we found today.'

'Beyond all possible doubt?'

'Don't ask silly questions, Burma. This method's as reliable as fingerprints. We've got the best police laboratory there is, and their verdict's unequivocal: this is the gun that was used to do in your friend. Just between ourselves, that's what you've been suspecting, isn't it, ever since we found it in that fellow's kitchen?'

'Why should I have thought that? The calibre? There's more than one .32 knocking around.'

'True. And you didn't know the bullets we found in Colomer were foreign. That's what led us off on the wrong track and my idea that it might have been a political crime. I think I mentioned it to you.'

'Yes.'

'I should have realized international crooks like Eiffel Tower Joe and his friends always use this kind of weapon.'

'Eiffel Tower Joe?'

'Of course – you haven't heard the best part. What do you reckon your assailant's name was?'

'You're having me on. Look, Lyon may be a centre of

spiritualism, but don't tell me the dead come back to life for a bit of target practice.'

'No, Joe didn't kill Colomer. Colomer's murderer, and yours too, so to speak, was Paul Carhaix – at least if we rely on the army papers he was carrying. But I've more confidence in these little pictures here. They're more difficult to forge.'

He took two more from his collection.

'Let's go on with the family album. Next, the fingerprints taken from the body of Paul Carhaix, so called. Next again, some fingerprints taken from the police file on one Paul Jalome. He's got quite a record. Escape from prison. Breaking parole. A one-time member of Georges Parris's gang, later of Villebrun's gang too. The prints are the same. Sticks out a mile, doesn't it?'

I snapped my fingers in surprise. Bernier didn't give me time for any other reaction.

'Colomer must have identified him as the pearl thief's old accomplice – you remember his press cuttings. But I don't think that's the only reason he was killed. Jalome could easily have tried to get away. After all, there wasn't much Colomer could do. No, there's something else. The fact that Paul had also been a member of Villebrun the bank robber's gang. Villebrun was only recently released from prison, and we believe he might be out for revenge. What could be simpler than for him to give his old henchman a gun? That way Jalome avenges his boss and at the same time eliminates a witness embarrassing to himself. That might sound rather naïve reasoning. But criminals often are naïve – you know that as well as I do.'

'Quite. But why should one of them use a revolver in Perrache station, and his bare fists when he's all alone with me? Naïvety again?'

'The noise, Monsieur Burma, the noise.'

He picked up the revolver again.

'This attachment is a Hornby silencer. It minimizes both the sound of a detonation and the flash. Enough for some-one to be able to use a gun amid the din of a railway station, especially if there's a military band playing. But not enough to use in the open in the middle of the night. What's more, to tell you the honest truth, I don't think Carhaix or Jalome or whatever you like to call him chose Perrache deliberately as the ideal place. If you ask me he was following Colomer, and only shot him because he had to. I mean when he saw him running towards you calling your name, he thought he was going to tell you everything. So he shot him in desperation.'

'But what was Bob doing at the station?'

Bernier thumped the table impatiently.

'Surely the inquiry's established that already! He was running away. He was out of his league. He could have handled Jalome on his own, but with Villebrun thrown in it was too much. And he must have been clumsy and aroused their suspicions. So he decided the only way to get out alive was to hop it. At least for a while.'

'Where did Jalome call me from?'

'Not from the agency. Lafalaise is no longer under sus-picion, by the way.'

'Where *did* he call from?'

'From an empty flat near the agency. The tenants were only away for a little while, so the phone wasn't discon-nected. Jalome couldn't risk using a call-box, as he'd have had to show his papers for that. Knowing about this flat he broke in and did his dirty work from there. The lock was almost intact. He was a pro.'

I gave him time to bask in my admiration. Then:

'So everything's quite clear now?'

'Absolutely.'

He preened himself. To give him his due he really had worked fast.

'So the case is closed?' I said.

He grunted.

'As far as Carhaix, alias Jalome, is concerned, yes. But we're still looking for Villebrun. As soon as we were sure he was behind Colomer's murder we started questioning a petty thief who's an ex-accomplice of his. He admitted that Jalome was one of his old partners in crime. But since then we haven't got a word out of him. He just keeps saying he doesn't know what his old boss is up to.'

He looked at his watch and gave an unpleasant laugh.

'It's still not very late. They've got all night to persuade him. Perhaps he'll decide to talk in the morning. A drop more coffee?'

'Yes. And a whole lump of sugar if you don't mind.'

He poured the coffee and put in the sugar without demur, whistling complacently to himself. A happy man. I wouldn't have dented his euphoria for anything.

I woke up in the hospital after a few hours of troubled sleep. It wasn't the Commissaire's ersatz coffee that had kept me awake. I hadn't liked to disturb Marc in the early hours, and Bernier had dropped me back at the hospital. Despite his presence the doorman complained that there didn't seem to be much wrong with me. And in the morning I was just getting ready to prove he was right by disappearing again when the nurse told me I was wanted urgently in the office.

'It's not to give you a ticking off,' she said, seeing me hesitate.

She was incapable of telling a lie, so I made my way to the office. A sort of NCO was waiting for me there, chewing on a pen with complete disregard for hygiene.

'You're all right now, it seems,' he said.

'Yes.'

'You live in Paris?'

'Yes.'

'Get your stuff ready then. You're going back this evening. The Germans are allowing a special repatriation train that'll be going through Lyon tonight. You'll be on it. Here are your demob papers and two hundred francs.'

'But I—'

'Don't tell me you don't want to go. It can't be because you like it here – we've hardly seen you in the place for more than two hours together.'

I explained it wasn't the hospital so much as the town that made me want to stay. Couldn't they delay my departure? I had a lot of things to see to. He said it wasn't his job to organize people's love lives, and if I wanted to stay on in Lyon I should have thought about it sooner. How was he to know what I wanted? And he couldn't change all the paperwork just for my benefit. If I liked Lyon so much I only had to go home and then get a pass to come back again.

'Your train's at twenty-two hundred hours,' he said. It was clear that bureaucracy was deaf and further protest was useless.

I made my way towards the nearest post office, determined to use my influential contacts. I showed my papers and asked to be put through to Commissaire Bernier. Then I told them to cancel the call. There were useful things to be done in the occupied zone, after all. I might just as well go back to Paris.

I went and told Marc Covet the news and had to give him a blow by blow account of my meeting with Bernier. It was all I could do to prevent him from writing a piece there and then. But I promised him more material that evening.

I spent most of the day chatting to some bartenders I knew who were doing well on the black market. I was looking for some Philip Morris cigarettes for Montbrison.

He'd been decent to me and I wanted to show my gratitude. But I couldn't find any anywhere, and had to make do with cigars. Cigars weren't his poison, but he accepted them graciously. I had to tell him the whole story too. He said it was wonderful at least twenty times.

'I hope to see you in Paris,' I said as I left.

'Yes. But when? I still haven't got my pass. I know a few people in the police, but no one senior enough to pull any strings. It drags on and on.'

'It looks as if I'm right to take advantage of the troop train then,' I said.

My last visit was to Gérard Lafalaise's office. Louise Brel looked embarrassed when she saw me.

'Don't worry,' I said as I held out my hand. 'I won't eat you.'

Then I went through to say goodbye to her boss, and called the Commissaire on his phone.

'We'll have to wait for our game of poker,' I said. 'Orders from the army – what's left of it. I've got to go back to Paris tonight. You don't need me, do you?'

'No.'

'Anything more from the purse snatcher?'

'We've had to suspend the interrogation.'

'No! . . . Doctor's orders, I suppose. For God's sake don't kill him!'

'His kind are tough! Bon voyage!'

By nine-thirty Marc Covet and I were pacing up and down a damply gleaming Platform 12. Marc was silent. I'd filled him up with yet more promises. The huge glass-roofed station was swept with gusts of an icy wind that threatened snow. It was too uncomfortable to stand about, but we weren't tempted by the buffet, which was ill-lit, badly heated and didn't have much to sell. So we tramped to and fro, shoulders hunched and collars turned up.

Eventually the special train drew in. It was a two-minute stop. I managed to find a seat.

'Au revoir,' said Marc. 'Remember me in your prayers.'

Part two
Paris

1 Getting in touch again

Reaching my front door was no easy matter. My concierge was waiting by the stairs, warned by a sixth sense of the exact time of my arrival. She handed me a bunch of letters which had been mouldering in her lodge since the end of the 'Phoney War' and told me she'd had the electricity and telephone reconnected. I had no choice but to go into the usual banalities about being a prisoner of war. Then I shot up to my flat on the third floor.

I made myself at home again more easily than I'd expected. I washed and shaved, got reacquainted with a trusty old bottle that had been waiting for me under the bed since September 1939, and picked up the phone.

How pleasant it was not to have to show my birth certificate beforehand, I thought as I dialled. I asked to speak to Inspector Faroux, and was told he wasn't in. Did I want to leave a message? I asked the operator to tell him Nestor Burma was back, and gave her my number. Then, as I hadn't slept on the journey, I went to bed.

Next day I bought an armful of papers and magazines on every possible subject: politics, literature, even fashion. I've a soft spot for women's magazines.

I spent the morning reading and waiting for a call from Faroux. It didn't come.

I learned from one elegant weekly that Dr Hubert Dor-cières had also been freed from the POW camp. The usual demob red tape had been cut for him, and he'd been in Paris for several days. The weekly was happy to inform its readers that the eminent surgeon, etc. It gave his address, which I noted down. I had mislaid Desiles's wife's address. Perhaps Dorcières would have it.

I looked through the pages dealing with politics, international and domestic, the war and the black market, and examined the small ads as I'd done for twenty years in the hopes of finding a request to contact a lawyer's office where I would learn something to my advantage. Such as a large bequest from a long-lost uncle. It was midday by now, so I put on a favourite old tweed suit, eccentric but not loud, and went out to lunch. Then I went home again and looked through the mail. At two o'clock the phone rang. It wasn't Florimond Faroux. It was the distant voice of Gérard Lafalaise.

'Our friend's had a slight accident. He'll be out of action for a few days,' he said. 'He was knocked over by one of the few cars still on the road.'

'He's not putting on an act, is he?'

'No. I'll call you when he's got over it. I can use my contacts to get information. As long as it's not too often.'

'Thanks. That'll give me time to get my strength back.'

I hung up and then dialled the Pointed Tower, headquarters of the C.I.D., again.

This time, after the usual preliminaries, my friend's voice came on, whistling through his moustache.

'You're in luck. I've just got in and was just about to leave again. Not even time to call you back. Yes, yes – I got your message.'

'Can we meet in – let's say an hour?'

'Quite impossible, old man. Not before tonight. I'm run off my feet. It's not urgent, is it?'

'That depends on you. I hope you got the letter about the rue de Lyon.'

'Yes.'

'Anything new on that subject?'

'No. As a matter of fact—'

'All right. I can wait. I can fill in time at the cinema. Let's fix a time to meet, though. How about nine o'clock at my place? It's nice and private. That all right? . . . Yes, it's heated. I've connected my electric fire to the meter next door.'

'All right. Being a prisoner of war seems to have changed you. You're very chatty.'

'That won't be Commissaire Bernier's opinion in the not-too-distant future.'

'Commissaire Bernier? Who's he?'

'A colleague of yours in Lyon, who envies the unemployed and is doing all he can to earn an early retirement.'

'And you're keeping him in the dark, eh?'

'And how! You know I can't stand policemen.'

'I'd better hang up,' he laughed. 'If one of my superiors overheard this conversation . . . See you tonight.'

'See you tonight, conformist.'

I used my free afternoon to look up the detectives who used to work for my agency. Roger Zavatter had been taken prisoner too. Jules Leblanc was dead. Louis Reboul, as a reservist, had suffered a fate somewhere between the two: he'd lost his right arm in one of the first engagements on the Maginot Line. He and I had an emotional reunion. I didn't mention Bob Colomer's death. I thought it best to keep that for another day. I left with promises to remember him if any small jobs came up. Just down the road was a non-stop cinema showing *Tempest*, with Michèle Hogan. I went in. It couldn't do me any harm.

'Hallo,' I said, as soon as Florimond Faroux's regulation

boots stepped on to my hall carpet. 'Yes, it's cold outside, there isn't any coal and we've lost the war. That's got that out of the way. Now for your questions. To avoid needless discussion, I was a prisoner at Sandbostel and went on a slimming cure of potatoes. It wasn't any worse than being in a mental hospital. Talking of which, how are you? I hope you're keeping as well as I am. There! That's about it, don't you think? Now take a seat and have a glass of red wine.'

Inspector Florimond Faroux of the Criminal Investigation Department was approaching forty with more speed than he'd ever shown chasing thieves. Which is saying a good deal. He was a tall gaunt man, but well built. His younger colleagues called him 'Grandpa' because of his grey moustache. Whatever the reason, he wore a peculiar and peculiarly unbecoming brown hat. He'd never managed to fathom my sense of humour, but punctuated our conversations with bursts of laughter which because of the law of averages were occasionally relevant. But all in all he was a good fellow, obliging and paternal. Or rather, grandpaternal. He listened disapprovingly to my cynical preamble, then shrugged, sat down, took off his hat and draped his moustache round a glass of wine.

'Now,' I said after I'd filled and lighted my pipe, 'what have you done for me?'

He coughed.

'Anyone who works with you gets used to outlandish assignments. But even so . . . Asking me to trail your ex-secretary . . . !'

'What do you mean? She's just an ordinary woman. She could go off the rails from one day to the next.'

'I suppose so. All the same, it did strike me as a bit much.'

'I hope that doesn't mean you haven't done anything about it.'

He raised a hand in protest.

'I've made out a report of sorts,' he said, 'but there's not much there.'

He plunged a hand into his vast pocket and brought out two typed sheets of paper. I read them with growing exasperation.

His 'report of sorts' was in fact very precise. Hélène Chatelain had been followed for two days and done nothing at all objectionable. She left home at eight-thirty in the morning, went straight to the Lectout Press Agency, had lunch in a restaurant at midday and went straight home at six. She didn't go out in the evening except on Thursday, when she went to the cinema. She spent from Saturday midday to Sunday evening at her mother's place. She hadn't been away once since the exodus in 1940. Was I on the wrong track?

But no stone must be left unturned, as my friend Bernier would say, though he overlooked whole quarries himself. And that's why I'd had Hélène Chatelain followed.

But these policemen, efficient professionals whose job it was to be suspicious, were telling me there was nothing doubtful about her behaviour. It was very discouraging. Or else Hélène was cleverer than I'd ever supposed. I decided I'd have to see her.

Faroux brought me down to earth by asking if everything was all right, and if I still wanted her followed. I answered yes to both questions. Then I showed him the photo of the prisoner who'd lost his memory.

'Do you know him by any chance?'

He laughed when he saw the number on his chest.

'You had mug-shots even out there, did you?'

'One of these days I'll tell you about all the other things we had out there. You'll be surprised. But for the moment, what do you make of that face?'

He gave me back the photograph.

'Nothing.'

'Never seen him before?'

'No.'

I let it go and handed him the fingerprints.

'I'd like you to see if these aren't already on your files.'

'Same bloke?'

'Same bloke as what?'

'The photo and the fingerprints – do they belong to the same person?'

'No,' I said. I'm a compulsive liar. 'But this is serious. I'd like an answer soon.'

'You're always in such a hurry,' he groaned, putting the fingerprints carefully away in his wallet. 'I'll do what I can. We can't keep up with the work at the moment.'

'No one's asking you to check it out yourself. Just as long as you don't mention my name to the dabs man. And another thing . . .'

I opened a drawer and showed him a sweet little automatic.

'I need a licence for this. It doesn't like being alone. It really only feels safe in my pocket.'

'Right.'

'Oh, and I may need to move around after dark. I'd like a pass.'

'Is that all?'

'Yes. You may go now.'

'I was just going to ask your permission,' he said, pouring some more wine. 'It's getting late.'

He emptied his glass in one and wiped his moustache. He started to get up, but suddenly stopped dead.

'That Commisssaire Bernier you mentioned – would he be Armand Bernier?'

Faroux gave me a description that did credit to his professional abilities.

'That's him,' I said. 'What's more, he's got a red face, he looks quite smart when he takes his raincoat off, and he's always putting his foot in it.'

Faroux began to laugh.

'I knew him a long time ago, when he was in Paris.'

He went on about Bernier for a good quarter of an hour, hoping to make me spill the beans.

2 The man who lost his memory

The clock struck nine. I gave it ten minutes, then picked up the phone and called up Lectout, the Readall Press Agency.

'Is Mlle Chatelain there?'

'No, monsieur, Mlle Chatelain won't be in for several days. She's got flu.'

I put on my coat and hat and went out into the cold morning air. Then I took the underground and didn't surface again until I reckoned it was completely light.

Before ringing the bell at my ex-secretary's flat I glued my ear to the keyhole. Not the kind of thing you'll find in a book of etiquette, but sometimes I've found it useful. And I must admit that the talents of most of my colleagues don't extend much farther. Anyhow, this time it wasn't any help: I couldn't hear a thing. So I rang. There was a sniff, a hoarse 'Who's there?' and then another sniff.

'It's me – Nestor Burma.'

A stifled exclamation.

'What! You, boss? Just a minute.'

A moment later the door opened and there stood Hélène Chatelain dabbing at a red nose with a tiny handkerchief. She was hermetically sealed in a dressing-gown over her pyjamas. Her mules didn't match, her hair wasn't combed and she had no make-up on. She wasn't quite so fetching as when she used to tan her charming chassis in the southern sun. But her body still gave off the same disturbing scent of cypress and powder, and despite the lack of make-up her face was as pretty as ever, with its fine black eyebrows and big grey eyes. She was clearly pleased to see me again. I was flattered.

'Come in!' she said. 'You're a great one for surprises. I won't kiss you, but it's the thought that counts.'

'Afraid I'll catch your cold?' I said.

'My God, is it as obvious as that?' she cried in alarm. 'No. It's just that it wouldn't be proper. Especially as you're in my bedroom . . . '

'Very good of you to let me in.'

'It's the only room in the flat that's heated,' she laughed. 'Don't get the wrong idea!'

She pushed a chair towards me and tidied the bedclothes. Then she lay down again and pulled up the covers. There was a row of medicine bottles within reach, and a teapot on a portable stove. It wasn't a diplomatic illness that was keeping her in her room. The hoarse voice she spoke in throughout our meeting was further proof.

'Would you like some tea?' she asked. 'It's the genuine article, and I've got some rum. Perhaps you could help yourself.'

I accepted. She blew her nose discreetly and then said:

'Come to get me to track down some octogenarian crook?'

She was light-hearted and poised. Not a sign of anxiety. I began to laugh.

'You're too modest. Don't you think I might just have come for the pleasure of seeing you? I've seen nothing but men since I was released, and I felt I'd like to look at a pretty face. Marc Covet, Montbrison and the rest are nice enough, but . . . '

'Marc? Have you seen him?'

'In Lyon. His paper's there now.'

'I knew the *Crépu* had moved away from Paris, but I didn't know where to. How is he?'

'Not too bad. A bit thin, like everyone else. Montbrison's the only one who keeps his weight up.'

'Montbrison?'

'Julien Montbrison. He's a lawyer. He came to the agency once, a long time ago. Don't you remember him? Rather fat. Wears a lot of rings.'

'No. I don't remember.'

'A pal of Bob's. A friend, to be more formal.'

'Oh . . . And what about Bob himself – what's become of him? I never hear from him.'

'Bob? His troubles are over. I saw him, just for a few seconds,' I said. 'He was murdered before my very eyes, in Lyon.'

She jerked upright in bed. Her pale face turned grey, and the rings seemed to darken under her eyes.

'Murdered!' she exclaimed. 'Is this a joke?'

'No. Colomer's dead.'

She stared at me intently, and I returned her stare. Even in that gloomy light I could see that though she was upset – Colomer had been well liked in the agency – she was showing only a natural distress. She wanted to know all the details, and I told her as much as I thought fit, pretending to share Bernier's conclusions. I set several traps for her as I spoke, but she didn't fall into any of them.

I took advantage of the fact that she was off balance to spring a real test on her, and suddenly asked her to look at the photo of 60202. But she just said in a perfectly ordinary voice:

'Who is it?'

'A fellow-prisoner of mine. I thought you knew him.'

'No, I don't. What made you think that?'

'Nothing,' I growled. 'You're about the fiftieth person I've shown it to.'

She shot me a mocking glance from under her long lashes.

'When shall I give in my notice at Readall's?'

'Oh, don't get the idea I'm working on a case. The Fiat Lux Agency's still dormant. The war's given it a real hammering. What with Leblanc dead, Zavatter in prison, Reboul wounded . . . And now Bob.'

She shook her head sadly. When she looked at me again, though, there was a light in her eyes. 'But you're still here, aren't you, boss? And still OK.'

'Yes . . . I'm still here.'

'Well, when you need me, just let me know.'

I put an end to this disappointing encounter, and left 60 rue de Lyon baffled and very bad tempered. Either my imagination had led me up a blind alley or the girl was making a fool of me. Neither possibility appealed to me much.

I holed up in a nearby café and waited with my eyes glued to her front door. But what was the point of this idiotic ploy? What was I waiting for? For Hélène to rush out and warn some unknown person that Burma was on the warpath? Or did I expect Colomer's killer to pay her a call?

At a nearby table a man was surreptitiously reading a paper and watching me. Sometimes he too looked across the street. Faroux's man. About as unobtrusive as an elephant at the Folies-Bergère. I was so angry I almost went over and told him not to bother, but I restrained myself.

I resigned myself to having wasted my time, left the café under his suspicious gaze, and spent the rest of the day browsing in every bookshop I came across.

I was nervous as I stood smoking my pipe in the broom-cupboard with a skylight that served Faroux as an office. The door opened and he came in.

On my return from dinner I had found a *pneumatique*

waiting for me. It said he'd tried without success to reach me by phone during the afternoon, and was too busy to go out again. Would I like to drop in at the Quai des Orfèvres at about half past nine? He'd identified the fingerprints.

'Ah! There you are,' he said with unusual brusqueness. 'I can only give you a few minutes. I'm on a very difficult case. Think yourself lucky I bother with you and your nonsense at all.'

I whistled.

'A noticeable drop in the temperature,' I said. 'What's wrong?'

'About the rue de Lyon,' he said, not answering my question. 'Your ex-secretary didn't go to work. Nothing special about that. Except that this morning someone seemed to be watching her house from the café opposite. What's more, he'd just come out of her building. He seemed in a filthy temper and didn't stay for long. My man was sorry he couldn't follow him.'

'Tell your man, first, to take some lessons in camouflage. Second, that he can still go after the suspect. It was me.'

Faroux was really cross now.

'And am I still supposed to keep up the surveillance? This is all completely against the regulations—'

'Go on with it all the same. You never know. It might get you promoted.'

'I doubt it.'

'What about the fingerprints?'

'Ah yes. Those. Some kind of a joke, is it? We coppers may make life a misery for people who're still alive. But the lengths you private eyes go to . . . ! Are you asking me to slap the bracelets on the chap these dabs belong to? That really would help my career!'

'No, that's not what I want. He's dead.'

Faroux almost exploded.

'So you knew? That's too much!'

'Yes, I knew.'

'And you got me poking around in our files looking for someone who's dead and buried. And did you know who he was?'

'No.'

His grey moustache was almost touching my face.

'You didn't know who it was?'

'I've already said I didn't. You're going to tell me.'

'With pleasure. The fingerprints belong to Georges Parris, international escape artist and pearl thief. Better known as Eiffel Tower Joe.'

3 The burglar

I jumped up, sending my chair spinning. My pipe flew out of my mouth and rolled across the floor. The picture of stupefaction.

'Eiffel Tower Joe?' I stuttered. 'Georges Parris?'

I grabbed Faroux by the lapels.

'Go and get the mug-shot album,' I shouted. 'Georges Parris didn't die in '38. He was still alive a month ago.'

Faroux was so stunned by this revelation that he did as I said without demanding any further explanation.

'Compare this photo with the one of Parris,' I said when he came back with his catalogue of criminals. I handed him the picture of the prisoner who'd lost his memory.

'But you told me—'

'Never mind what I told you. The man in the photo is the same one I took the prints from.'

Faroux put his head in his hands.

'But, good Lord,' he wailed, almost ready to give up the whole thing, 'it can't be the same man!' He looked at me helplessly. 'Is it possible that for the first time in the history of scientific research, fingerprints don't—'

'Pull yourself together, Faroux. You've studied them, haven't you? How many features do they have in common?'

'Seventeen. The maximum.'

'On each finger?'

'On each finger.'

'So there's no mistake,' I said. 'Our gangster is No. 60202.'

'It can't be the same man,' he insisted, no longer comparing the two pictures.

'But it is. It's the same man not *despite* the fact that he looks different, but *because* he looks different. Don't stare at me like that! I'm not mad – I've just got more imagination than . . . some people. Calm down and look closely. The general shape of the face hasn't changed. But apart from the scar, the individual features have been modified. The mouth is smaller, and there's an artificial dimple in the chin. Georges Parris had a snub nose. 60202's is straight, and the nostrils are narrower. As for the ears, they lie close against the head, and the antitragus is flat instead of protuberant.'

'You're right,' he admitted after examining them for a moment. Then, realizing the implications, he gave vent to his fury against the surgeons responsible.

'How is it the body was identified as his in Cornwall in '38?' I asked.

'Oh! The corpse was half-eaten by crabs . . . Still, Scotland Yard did identify it.'

'You mean it was wishful thinking on the part of the British police!'

'Anyway, after his death, genuine or otherwise, no one heard any more about him.'

'He intended to retire and live off his income. That's why he staged his own death, then put himself in the hands of a top surgeon.'

Faroux cursed the unscrupulous medic, then asked me to explain myself. Having recovered myself and lit my pipe again, I gave him a detailed account of what had happened, omitting all reference to Michèle Hogan's double. The Inspector plucked thoughtfully at his moustache.

'Let's go over it again,' he said. 'You meet Georges Parris in the POW camp. He's lost his memory . . . Was that genuine?'

'Absolutely.'

'Just before he dies, he has a miraculous lucid interval and says: "Hélène . . . 120 rue de la Gare".'

'And I say "Paris?", and he thinks I'm saying his name and nods. So there's no connection with the rue de la Gare in the 19th arrondissement. And anyway, number 120 doesn't exist.'

'Right. So when you get to Lyon you witness Bob Colomer's murder, and he dies with the same mysterious address on his lips. Do you think he'd found out Georges Parris was still alive?'

'Yes, I do. It's the only thing that could link the two affairs together.'

'I agree . . . Soon after Colomer's death you hit on the idea that 120 rue de la Gare might be 60 rue de Lyon. Right. And to find out about the kind of life your assistant had been leading in Lyon, you go to a local private detective. His secretary talks too much, and one of Georges Parris's old gang tries to do you in. According to Commissaire Bernier, Jalome killed Colomer too. But you don't agree about that, do you?'

'No.'

'Why not?'

'Because Jalome was such a careful type. I'm not talking only about how spick and span his flat was. I mean how few papers there were in his wallet. I don't believe anyone as careful as that would leave a revolver lying around. I'm convinced that between midnight and three-thirty, when we got to his flat, someone else went there.'

'Do you have any proof?'

'No. Only theories.'

'And who do you think the other visitor was?'

'Colomer's killer. The man who put Jalome on to me. Suppose he was waiting not far from the Pont de la Boucle. When he didn't see his henchman come back . . . No, he must have heard the splash and seen us walk out of the ambush as large as life. He didn't know how much I knew, and Jalome's flat would obviously be searched sooner or later. So to do away with any compromising evidence he went there and cleaned up – he must have a key. He hid the gun that killed Bob Colomer in an obvious place, to throw suspicion on Jalome. You couldn't trace the real owner from the revolver itself. It's foreign, and it was smuggled into the country and bought illegally – it'll soon be impossible to get ammunition for it. So he had every reason to ditch it.'

'God all bloody mighty,' Faroux exploded. 'I don't know what you're doing in Paris, then. If your argument holds water your killer's in Lyon.'

'I had no choice – I was forced to come. But I left instructions with Gérard Lafalaise, and anyway my guess is that we'll find the solution to the riddle somewhere in the occupied zone. In Paris or elsewhere.'

'What makes you think that?'

'Intuition, first of all. Don't laugh. It's because people like you and Bernier have no intuition that you flounder about so pathetically. For example, it was intuition that told me to take 60202's fingerprints after he died. I'd noticed how casually he registered them for the Germans, as though he was used to it. All the others were nervous. It's only a detail, but my method is made up of details—'

'And of manhandling witnesses . . . '

'Why not? Every little helps. Where was I?'

'You were saying why you think the solution to the mystery lies in the occupied zone.'

'Oh yes. So, first my intuition. Then the fact that Colomer was preparing to cross the line. Remember, I've never believed for a second that he was running away. That was Commissaire Bernier's idea. If Colomer had found out that Carhaix was Jalome, or in other words Eiffel Tower Joe's accomplice – and Villebrun's too, though I don't see how that could have interested him – all he had to do to protect himself was tell the police. Finally, I don't think I've wasted my time coming back to dear old Paris. I've been able to identify the man without a memory – and take a closer look at Hélène Chatelain.'

'What's she got to do with all this?'

'I saw her this morning, and my impression is she's got nothing to do with it at all. But I could be wrong. That's why I think we should go on keeping an eye on her. But I'm afraid I was trying to read more into an address than was really there. Trying to be too clever, much as I hate to admit it. My famous equation – 120 rue de la Gare = 60 rue de Lyon – could be completely wrong. 120 rue de la Gare may mean just 120 rue de la Gare, no more and no less. Of course that explanation was far too simple for me! But there's no shortage of streets called "rue de la Gare" in France – there must be one in every town. As for the name Hélène, I was wrong to get carried away by that too.'

'I'll go on having her watched all the same,' said the Inspector doggedly.

I couldn't help laughing. Cops were all the same. The more wrong a line of inquiry proved, the more obstinately they stuck to it.

We were silent for a bit. Faroux seemed to have forgotten he could only spare me a few minutes.

I spoke first.

'Could you get me an ordnance survey map of the Château-du-Loir area? The army's cartographical office is closed, and I've been trying to find one all afternoon.'

'I can get it for you by tomorrow. What do you want it for?'

'It's an idea that's been nagging at me for a long time. That's why I didn't try to get my stay in Lyon extended. I want to have a look at the area where Georges Parris was picked up and taken prisoner. Maybe I'll find some clues. A rue de la Gare, for example.'

'Do you need any help? Want me to talk to the chief about it?'

'Not for the moment. I'll try to make out on my own. First I want to find exactly where he was captured. I don't even know if that's possible.'

'You haven't got much to go on.'

'The photograph should help.'

'The local people were hiding in their cellars when all that kerfuffle was going on. If you think they're going to recognize all the soldiers who happened to pass through . . .'

'Parris wasn't a soldier. A soldier trying to pass for a civilian gets rid of his uniform first, not his underclothes. I think it's more likely that someone – I don't know why – stuck a uniform on him. Clear as mud, eh? Haven't had a brain-teaser like this for a long time. A nice easy little job for someone just back from POW camp in delicate health. But if I ferret about patiently in the Château-du-Loir area I might just find the end of Ariadne's thread.'

Faroux shook his head.

'A thankless task,' he said.

'I believe in my star,' I said stubbornly, getting up. 'Dynamite Burma's star. Pre-war quality.'

He looked at me in silence, as if this wasn't the moment to rub me up the wrong way. As we shook hands he suddenly thought of something.

'Wait a minute – I was forgetting your gun permit.'

He handed it over.

'Thanks,' I said, 'I was sure you'd turn up trumps. Feel my pocket.'

'Are you mad?' he exclaimed. 'You're a walking arsenal!'

'Nothing went wrong,' I said. 'And now' – tapping the permit – 'nothing will.'

'Your star again, eh?'

'That's right.'

The first snowflakes were falling into the river. It was going to be a picture-postcard Christmas. I dived into the underground to avoid it. Inspector Florimond Faroux might have doubts about my star, but it existed all the same. Half an hour later there was proof of it, in the form of a charming and unexpected burglar who turned up at just the right moment.

Unlike my friend Emile C., I don't usually sing as I go up the stairs, especially when I get back late. Just as well, because otherwise my nocturnal visitor would have heard me coming and made himself scarce.

When I reached the door I noticed it wasn't shut. A faint ray of light from a lamp on my desk shone through the crack, and I could just make out the shape of a shortish man tinkering with the lock on my desk. I took out my revolver, burst in, slammed the door behind me and switched on the light.

'Don't waste your time,' I said. 'There's nothing there but unpaid bills.'

The man started, dropped the implement he was using and turned round, white as a sheet. A big bundle lay at his feet, no doubt containing the swag from other flats in the building, most of whose tenants had fled to the unoccupied zone. He raised his arms slowly in the classic 'hands up' posture, revealing that three fingers were missing on his right hand. And although his cap was pulled down over his eyes, the rest of his face was that of a typical crook. He let out a bloodcurdling oath. His voice was hoarse, and he spoke out of the corner of his mouth.

'It's a fair cop,' he said.
I started, and gave a triumphant laugh.
'Well, Bébert,' I said. 'How's tricks?'

4 *The lonely house*

Under the peak of his cap he blinked. He didn't recognize me. I briefly refreshed his memory. He was already pale with fear, but he went even paler with amazement. His mouth grew more twisted than ever and he vented his astonishment in a graphic style I couldn't attempt to reproduce. I shoved him towards a chair and he sank limply on to it.

'I'm not going to hand you over to the police,' I said.

By now he was sipping a glass of wine generously supplied by his intended victim, and beginning to get over his surprise.

'No. In a minute you're going to put back everything you've taken and we'll forget all about your moment of weakness.'

'Oh, thank you . . . ' he began, all ready to pour out excuses.

'Don't take me for a fool,' I cut in. 'I'm not lecturing *you*, so spare me the sobstuff. I've got better things to do than listen to your lies.'

'Whatever you say.'

'You remember the chap who died in the camp hospital? We were both there at the time. The one who couldn't remember anything. You called him "the Blob".'

'Yeah.'

'You were there when he was captured too, if what you told me was true.'

'Yeah.'

'Would you recognize the place?'

'I expect so. But it's a long way away.'

'I know it's not in the Place de l'Opéra! Château-du-Loir, wasn't it?'

'Yeah.'

'We're going there tomorrow.'

Bébert didn't make any objections. He didn't understand what it was all about, but he thought himself lucky to be let off so lightly.

I started to telephone all over the place, trying to reach Florimond Faroux. I finally succeeded and told him I had to have two tickets for Château-du-Loir the following day. As far as I was concerned, there was no such thing as a full train. He must try and manage it. Yes, my star had done it again. I'd been reunited with an old friend who'd been there when Georges Parris was captured, and he was willing to take me to the very spot. I had the utmost difficulty preventing Faroux from sending us two guardian angels to look after us on the trip. But I managed it. Then I called Louis Reboul's old number, on the off-chance. I was lucky; it was still connected. He was half asleep when he answered.

'Burma here. Set your alarm for four-thirty, and be ready to come and stay in my flat from five o'clock on. I've got to go away all of a sudden, and I need someone to take an important call from the provinces. I shan't see you tomorrow, so here are your instructions. Are you awake enough to understand what I say, or should I leave you a note?'

'I'm wide awake, boss!'

It was quite true. He was as bright as a button, so glad was he not to have been forgotten.

'Go on – I'm writing it down,' he said.

I told him what he had to do.

'Now, it's just you and me, M. Bébert,' I said when I'd hung up. 'I must try and get some sleep, and as I don't want you clearing off I'm going to tie you up.'

He protested and said I was being mean. He offered me his word of honour. Meanwhile I tied him up by the wrists and ankles, laid him down on the sofa and threw a blanket over him. He must have been a fatalist at heart, because he was asleep in no time. But I tossed and turned all night, and had to get up several times to make sure the booze I keep for special occasions hadn't evaporated. But it only made me more nervous than ever.

My tobacco pouch was in my hand throughout the journey, either filling my pipe or doling out tobacco to my companion. This irritated me after a while: I was afraid he was taking me for a sucker. So I asked him why he couldn't buy his own tobacco, like everybody else.

'What with?' he whined. He fumbled in his pocket and took out two francs. All that was left of his demob hand-out.

I shrugged.

'You could collect cigarette butts off the floor.'

He said he wasn't too proud for that, but the corridor of a train wasn't as good as a street. This gives some idea of our general level of conversation. I heaved a sigh of relief when we reached Château-du-Loir.

I booked a double room in a second-class hotel. My companion didn't make too bad an impression on the staff, as I'd lent him an overcoat: it was too long for him, but less threadbare than the one he'd been wearing the day before. He'd also replaced his filthy cap with my béret, and I'd made him shave. The only problem was his habit of speaking out of the corner of his mouth, but as he wasn't very talkative . . . Before setting off I phoned Reboul and

gave him my address, and asked the hotel manager if there
was a rue de la Gare in the locality. He said there wasn't.

'Let's go, then,' I said, clapping Bébert on the back. 'See
this packet of shag? It's yours when we find the place.'

He pulled a face, went and stood in the middle of the
street to get his bearings, then shot off in a south-westerly
direction with me after him.

There was an unpleasantly chilly wind blowing and a
threat of snow in the grey sky. The streams were covered
with a thick layer of ice, and the frozen earth rang beneath
our boots. From a distance the black, leafless copses looked
like bundles of sticks tied together and abandoned in the
middle of the fields. From time to time a colony of rooks
would rise up from among the trees, black specks against
the grey. How desolate the scene was now compared with
the same landscape as it basked in the June sun. I wondered
with growing anxiety whether Bébert would be able to
recognize the place we were looking for.

Time passed, and there was no joyous exclamation from
the burglar to show he'd won his packet of shag. Night fell
so quickly we only just had time to turn round and make
our way back to the hotel. Our feet, hands and faces were
frozen. The cabbage soup the hotel served us was very
welcome. I gave Bébert a quarter of his tobacco. He'd
earned it. It wasn't his fault he hadn't found the place.

The next day we put away a substantial breakfast before
we went on with our search. A good thing about the country
was that it wasn't too hard hit by restrictions. The hotel
owner was only too delighted to have any guests at all, and
couldn't do enough for us. Was the wine all right? Were
we sure the bread wasn't too black? Were we generally
satisfied?

'Beyond our wildest dreams,' I said with my mouth full.
'But I'd be even more pleased if I could get hold of a fellow
I was a prisoner of war with. He's come into a fortune but

he doesn't know about it. It's my job to trace people like that,' I confided, showing him the photo of 60202.

He looked at it carefully and handed it back without a flicker of interest.

'Did he live round here?'

'I believe so. Doesn't the photo ring any bells?'

'No. Mind you, I've only been here three months. Old Combettes would have been able to tell you better.'

'Who's he?'

'A poacher. He knew everyone for ten miles round.'

'Where can I find him?' I said excitedly.

'In the churchyard,' he said. 'And he's not the sexton.'

I was about to curse with disappointment when Bébert got in before me.

'That's it,' he cried, dropping his fork and twisting his mouth like a corkscrew, 'I've got it! You can hand over the tobacco right now. Combettes – La Ferté-Combettes. I remember seeing it on a signpost about ten minutes after they nabbed me!'

'Is there a village called that in these parts?' I asked.

The hotel owner was so transfixed by the corkscrew he could hardly take his eyes off it. But he eventually turned to me.

'Yes, monsieur,' he said. 'Four miles away.'

'How do you get there?'

'There used to be a bus. But now you have to walk.'

'Tell us the way,' I said. He obligingly did so, and we struck out into the country. The wind had dropped and been replaced by snow. But I was almost happy. I was approaching my goal . . . I rubbed my hands, but not because of the cold.

By the time we reached La Ferté-Combettes the snow had started to settle. It was a tiny village: three higgledy-piggledy houses, a church, and a few scattered farms. Bébert examined the ground like a gun dog. Suddenly, his tail went up and he was off, telling me to follow. All his indecision had vanished. He pointed to a house with a thin wisp of smoke rising up from the chimney.

'I recognize that farm,' he said, 'The one with the crooked barn. That was our first stop. There should be a pond behind it.'

We squelched on a bit, then climbed up on to a bank. There was the pond, sure enough, its frozen surface beginning to disappear beneath the snow.

'It's in the bag,' said Bébert.

He turned into a winding path, and after a moment pointed triumphantly to a signpost marked 'La Ferté-Combettes, ¾ mile.' We went on and entered a small wood.

'The wood they nabbed us in is a bit further on,' he said.

'Never mind that,' I interrupted. 'I'm looking for the one the Blob came out of.'

'This is it.'

'Are you sure?'

'Quite sure.'

He went on a little way, then spun round and faced me.

'We were coming along here on our way to the farm. The Blob came out of here.'

'Good.'

I plunged into the wood, followed by Bébert demanding his tobacco. I stopped and gave it to him.

The wood was larger and denser than I'd expected. I pressed eagerly forward through a layer of fallen leaves, twigs and undergrowth. It was madness to look for clues in a place like this, six months after the event. But I kept going, and suddenly my efforts and my belief in my intuition were rewarded. We came to a house standing alone in a little clearing.

Weeds were closing in all round it, and it gave off a terrible aura of suffering and sadness. Most of the front of the house was overgrown with ivy, which completely obscured one of the first-floor windows. The shutters were closed, and a carpet of leaves showed through the snow on the steps. The iron gate screeched as we entered the garden; the front door creaked when I pushed it open with my foot. Inside the house we were met by a sickening smell of mildew and decay.

I switched on my torch. We were in a hallway with four doors leading off it: one to the kitchen, one to a kind of store-room, one to a large sitting-room and one to a sort of library. There was no electric light. Large oil lamps hung from the ceilings, and we found tins of paraffin in one of the cupboards. Love of the simple life hadn't extended, however, to the matter of central heating. Every room had one or two radiators, fed by a boiler we found later in the cellar. The massive chimney-pieces in the library and sitting-room were purely decorative. Or were they? In the fireplace in the library there was a heap of ashes and half-burnt logs. A wicker armchair had been drawn up in front of the hearth. My torch wasn't very powerful, so I asked Bébert to open the window. The result wasn't blinding, but I could now see all round the room.

The first thing my eye lighted on was a calendar showing the date: June 21st. I've noticed that almost everyone's first reaction when they see a calendar that's not up to date is to make it so. This one hadn't been touched since the twenty-first of June, so I was probably the first person who'd seen it since then. *Someone had lit a fire in this room on June 21st 1940.* I looked from the calendar to the chair. Whoever drew it up so close must really have felt the cold. Then I let out a yell. Lying on the floor around the chair were bits of cord.

Bébert was following my advice of the day before and prowling round picking up cigarette ends. I interrupted him.

'What date were you captured?'

'What, again? The 21st of June.'

'Is that the day you met the Blob?'

'Yes.'

'What was the matter with him? Didn't you say his feet were hurting him?'

'Yes. A real mess. Burned to bits. Must have been trying to do the fire dance!'

Yes. A strange kind of fire dance he'd been made to perform, Eiffel Tower Joe. There was no doubt that this must be Georges Parris's house, as I had plenty of opportunity to confirm in the hours that followed. Apart from the complete sets of classics, which were only there for show, their pages still uncut, all the books lying in the library reflected the gangster's own particular interests: pornography, law and criminology. There was a revealing collection of newspapers, too: he liked gloating over accounts of his own exploits.

Inside one of the books I found a photograph. It was of a young girl who could have been Michèle Hogan's twin sister. Apart from that, nothing of interest. That didn't surprise me. Crooks don't usually keep archives of incriminating evidence.

I had another look at the chair. On the left of the back, at about the height of the cheek of a person sitting in it, there was a strange kind of dent or scratch. Yet although it was covered with dust the chair was new. Bébert, who'd finished harvesting butt ends by now, watched in amazement as I examined it all over with a pocket magnifying glass. All I found was a tiny piece of what looked like glass, trapped between two bits of the wicker where the seat met the back. I dug it out with my knife and put it away in my wallet.

After closing the shutters again, we left this sinister and tragic scene. What with the isolation and the noise of the war raging all round – the boom of heavy artillery and the chatter of machine-guns – no one could have heard the gangster's cries of pain. He'd obviously been subjected to a form of third-degree torture resurrected for the occasion from the eighteenth century.

Now the whole countryside was covered with snow, and a bitter wind had got up. It wasn't the weather for hanging about, but I knocked at the door of the first house we came to. I couldn't have made a better choice. After a quarter of an hour spent first soothing a very fierce dog and then reassuring his owner – a sprightly old man who could only have been a poacher – I came by the following information:

The lonely house was called 'The Retreat' and belonged to somebody called Péquet. The old man identified Parris's photo as him. Monsieur Péquet was an eccentric who lived on his own, didn't mix with the people in the village and never had any visitors. He had come to live there in 1939. A couple called M. and Mme Mathieu (the old man was the husband) had 'done' for him, but on the morning of June 20th 1940 (the Mathieus remembered the date because a relative of theirs had died the day before), the man who'd arranged for them to work for M. Péquet in 1939 came to see them. He brought them the personal effects they'd left in the house and paid them three months' wages, telling them M. Péquet wouldn't be needing their services any longer as he'd decided to go back to the Midi. They weren't surprised. It was quite understandable. The guns had been getting closer since the day before, and the local squire had decamped long ago.

Old Mathieu did his best to describe the man who had seemed to be in charge of Péquet's affairs. But descriptions weren't his strong point, so I gave up, and Bébert and I went back to the hotel. Despite the horrific visions conjured up by 'The Retreat', I was humming a tune to myself as we went along.

I called in at the station to find out the times of the trains back to Paris, then we did justice to a meal that combined tea and dinner. Afterwards I settled up with Bébert. He'd earned the two hundred francs I gave him. As I handed them over he was dismantling his butts and collecting the tobacco in a cone made from a page from a catalogue he'd found on the gangster's desk. My generosity left him speechless. Not to be outdone, he offered me a handful of cigarette ends.

5 Rue de la Gare

I got back to my flat just before the curfew and found Reboul still holding the fort. He was sitting within reach of the telephone champing a toothpick.

'Evening, boss,' he said, holding out his left hand, or rather the hand that was left. 'I called your hotel in Château-du-Loir, but you'd already gone.'

'Oh, so the message arrived? What did it say?'

'Suspicious fellow, your caller, isn't he? I've written our conversation down. I'll read it to you – you'd never he able to understand my scribble. Here goes: "Hallo – is that M. Nestor?" "No, M. Nestor isn't here at the moment? Is that M. Gérard?" "Yes." "This is M. Reboul from the Fiat Lux Agency. I've been waiting here especially to take your call." "Right. Tell M. Nestor his friend's got over the accident. It turns out it wasn't serious, and he's catching the train to Paris this evening. He'll be there between half-past nine and ten tomorrow morning, unless there's a derailment." '

'Perfect,' I said. 'I want you to go and wait for him at the station. Tail him and let me know his address. I've got a photo for you to identify him by.'

I took out a press cutting.

'Inspector Faroux phoned too, just after I called Château-du-Loir,' said Reboul. 'He wants you to phone him right away.'

'Well, he'll have to wait. I'm going to get some sleep, and I strongly advise you to do the same. You'll need your wits about you tomorrow.'

I slept like a babe, and next morning while my assistant made his way to the station I went to the National Library to consult various yellowing periodicals. I concentrated particularly on *Crime and Police*, a mine of information on criminals great and small. Returning home quite pleased with my morning's work, I found Reboul standing out on the pavement in a very different state.

'I spotted your fellow all right,' he said sheepishly, 'but I lost him in the Métro. It's all my fault. I'm useless. Anyone'd think I'd lost my brain, not just my arm.'

He told me the whole story. His prey had escaped while he changed a ten-franc note at the ticket counter.

'I should have bought a book of tickets beforehand. A five-year-old would have thought of that.'

'Don't worry,' I said consolingly as I scratched my head. 'I'm not putting out any flags about your efforts, but I'm not in the habit of chewing war veterans up, either. Just tell me this: did he realize he was being followed and shake you off deliberately, or was it just an unfortunate combination of circumstances?'

'He didn't suspect a thing, boss. I'm not saying that was because I was clever. He just didn't seem to be expecting anything. It was a piece of cake. If it hadn't been for . . .'

'Forget it. From what you say it might still work out all right. It's quite possible he'll come and see me.'

Reboul went off with his tail between his legs; I sat down to do some phoning. After a few unsuccessful attempts I got through to Faroux. As soon as he heard my expedition to Château-du-Loir hadn't been a waste of time he interrupted excitedly.

'Don't move,' he said. 'I'll be right over.'

'I thought you were snowed under with work,' I said.

But he didn't hear. He was probably already on his way. I smiled as I lit my pipe. If even the placid Florimond was getting interested, things really were moving.

Just as my pipe went out the front-door bell rang. It couldn't be the Inspector so soon. It was Marc Covet.

He hurried over to the radiator. 'The *Crépu* chose a fine time to move back to Paris,' he said.

'Oh, you're going to work from here again, are you?'

'Yes. It's been on the cards for a few months, and now it's done. Brrh!'

'Quite,' I agreed. 'But I don't suppose the weather's much better in Lyon. Any news from there?'

Marc pulled a face and sat down.

'That's a strange business,' he said. 'If it wasn't true it'd made first-class fiction. Those Lyon policemen! Do you know what they did? They're so hidebound they sent a summons to a corpse. Our friend Carhaix-Jalome, no less . . . '

He paused for effect.

'Go on!'

'The day before yesterday Commissaire Bernier was informed that a policeman had left a summons at the dead man's flat, ordering him to come in to the local station. And what do you think he'd done? He'd committed the post-mortem crime of breaking the black-out regulations. On the night of the 15th to the 16th. The same night he attacked me and got paid out in his own coin. But at two o'clock that morning, when the man on patrol said he saw a light in Carhaix's flat, Carhaix was in the river, wasn't he?'

'Had been for about an hour and a half.'

'That's what Bernier told the policeman. But the cop's coming up to retirement, and he's not sure now that he didn't make a mistake about the time. Even about the flat the light was in, and the floor it was on.'

'Very interesting. If he did make a mistake about the time, it was our light he noticed. We had a close shave.'

'And if he didn't make a mistake?' said Marc.

I laughed.

'You're a big boy – draw your own conclusions! Between the time Carhaix fell in the river and the time we searched his flat, someone else went there. You've just proved it. Thanks.'

I knew he'd ask questions, so I created a diversion by offering him some rum.

'Mineral water, tap water or fruit juice,' he said. 'Nothing else.'

'Are you on the wagon?' I asked.

He paced round the room.

'Haven't you noticed anything?'

'A slight limp. Had an accident?' I said, laughing.

'Supposing I had? Is that so funny? . . . But no – it's the Pernod. The restrictions on drink came just in time. Saved my life. I must have alcoholic rheumatism or something. I haven't had an attack of it for a couple of years – I thought I'd got rid of it. But ouch! It got me in the train last night. Give me a glass of water. And don't have a real drink in front of me. It'd be too cruel.'

The door bell rang loudly and saved me from this dilemma.

'Who is it – the bailiff?' asked Marc politely.

'No. A lady who's teaching me strip poker,' I said. 'You'd be in the way.'

'I get it,' he said, standing up and wincing. 'I'm at the Hôtel des Arts in the rue Jacob. Don't forget me.'

'Wouldn't dream of it.'

I opened the door and almost got kicked on the shins. Florimond Faroux, tired of his bell sonata, was about to go into action with his feet.

'Is this your lady friend?' Marc chuckled. 'She might have shaved.'

He limped off downstairs.

The Inspector came in and sat on the radiator. It was popular tonight.

'Who's the lame duck?'

'A reporter.'

'Looks a right little crook to me.'

'The two things aren't mutually exclusive,' I said.

But we'd wasted enough time. I told him about the results of my investigations at Château-du-Loir, and the discoveries I'd made since.

'Makes you think, doesn't it?' I said. 'If we add it all up we get something like this: Georges Parris is tortured to make him confess something. The torturers use a method from the dark ages and slowly burn the soles of his feet. But instead of coughing up he loses his memory.'

Faroux looked at me in astonishment. I got up and took a book off the shelves.

'This is a treatise on sleep by a university professor,' I said. 'Listen. "When a person is in danger or subjected to great stress, he tends to sham dead or go to sleep to protect himself from painful reality. This 'escape into sleep' has been observed by a number of researchers. Take the case of the business man who received bad news by telephone and went to sleep with the receiver still in his hand. Or the young man who showed signs of extreme fatigue because he couldn't get on with his father. His father only had to come into the room for him to fall asleep. Then there's the highly intelligent woman who nods off whenever she's frustrated. When her singing lessons go badly, for instance. And the candidate in an oral exam who hasn't done enough work and drifts off to avoid having to answer the questions. And so on." '

I shut the book.

'It could be this same psychological phenomenon that made Eiffel Tower Joe lose his memory,' I said. 'He may have been tortured over a long period. The two servants were dismissed on the 20th, and there were signs in the house that someone had camped there. So Eiffel Tower Joe, alias Georges Parris, afraid he might give his secret away in spite of himself, might have fallen by a kind of defence mechanism into a state of amnesia so traumatic it became permanent. Only later, on his death-bed, was the process reversed. And I'm ready to bet that the first words he spoke when his memory came back were the ones his torturers couldn't get out of him: "120 rue de la Gare . . ." Not a very lucky address to know about, it seems to me.'

Faroux snorted.

'Very ingenious, as usual. But I'm not in a position to contradict you. There's still a lot that needs explaining. Perhaps we should get a search warrant to go over the house, and get a statement from the domestics. And that means bringing the Chief into it. Seriously, Burma, we can't go on keeping this to ourselves much longer. There've been developments while you've been away. I came specially to tell you about them, but so far I haven't been able to get a word in edgeways.'

'What kind of developments?'

'Were you still thinking your ex-secretary's in the clear? Because I'm afraid you were right first time there, too. She still hasn't gone back to work, but yesterday she went out. She was tailed to the Porte D'Orléans, where she obviously intended to take a bus. But they were all full, so she waved down a taxi-cycle. My man heard her giving the address: "It's not far – rue de la Gare". And the contraption set off in the direction of Montrouge and disappeared. My chap couldn't requisition another bike as he would have done if he'd been on regular duty. So he phoned me and went back to the rue de Lyon. Mlle Chatelain got home late in the evening. I've put more men on to watching her, but I was waiting for you to get back to see what else to do. I warn you I'm determined to do something.'

'So am I,' I said. 'We're a right pair of fire-crackers. But give me a day or two before you let your boss in on this . . . Now let's go and see the young lady.'

'I've got a car outside,' said the Inspector.

'Do you want to sink me with my concierge for ever?'

When we got to the rue de Lyon, Hélène was out. Her concierge thought she must have been using her last day's sick leave to do some shopping. So we went to the bar over the road, where one of Faroux's detectives sat waiting for retirement.

'Martin's followed the bird,' he said elegantly. 'Nothing can have gone wrong or he'd have phoned.'

There was nothing to do but sit it out, so we went and parked the car where it wasn't likely to be spotted and came back and had a few beers. The alcohol content wasn't enough to cheer us up.

At eight o'clock, when it was already dark, a man with a face like a horse appeared. Martin. Faroux plied him with questions. He'd just followed 'the bird' – he called her that too – from the Samaritaine to the Galeries Lafayette, and from there to the Printemps. He'd had a bellyful of department stores.

'Let's go,' I said, 'and if I rough her up a bit just look the other way.'

Hélène opened the door as soon as I said it was me. But she looked surprised when she saw my companion. I got straight to the point.

'Listen, sweetie, let's all put our cards on the table. The police have been following you for the last few days because I asked them to. We'll talk about whether I was right or wrong another time. For the moment I want to ask you some questions. Try not to wriggle out of them. You'll notice I'm chain-smoking my pipe. That means I'm really worked up.'

Her big grey eyes opened wide. She stepped back, knocked into the table and put a graceful hand to her bosom.

'You've been having me followed, boss?' she whispered. 'But why?'

'I'm asking the questions. So your flu's better, eh? Or else I presume you wouldn't have gone on a trip to the suburbs yesterday. I don't know exactly where in the suburbs, but I do know you went to a rue de la Gare. And that's an address I've been interested in for some time.'

I looked her straight in the eye. But all I could see there was the bewilderment caused by our visit.

'It's to do with Bob,' she said.

'Yes,' I observed sarcastically. 'Right first time.'

'I'm not asking you – I'm telling you,' she said firmly.

'Better still. It'll save time. So you went to the rue de la Gare because of Bob?'

'Yes.'

'Where exactly?'

'Châtillon.'

'And was it number 120 you went to?'

'No. Not 120. It was . . . oh dear, I don't remember the number. I don't think I ever knew it. It's a house Bob's parents rent, right at the end of the street.'

'So you went to see Bob's parents at some number you don't remember in the rue de la Gare?'

'Yes.'

'Don't try to make a monkey out of me, Hélène,' I said threateningly. 'You know me well enough to know you'd be the loser. I know their address. It was on a card they sent him in Lyon. The name of the house is Iris Villa, and it's in the rue Raoul-Ubac.'

'If you'd give me a chance I could explain. We're both

right. The rue Raoul-Ubac is the new name for the last part of the rue de la Gare. I didn't know that myself until yesterday. It was called "rue de la Gare" until the armistice. But I know the place because I went several times with Bob himself.'

She was obviously telling the truth. I kept relighting my pipe. I'd never been so agitated.

'And what did you go and see Bob's parents for?'

'I know them quite well, poor old things. And I went to offer my condolences. They'd only received an official notification of Bob's death. It was a terrible shock, especially for old Monsieur Colomer. He had to take to his bed. It really was bad luck. He'd only just got a new job as night-watchman at La Sade.'

I grabbed her by the blouse.

'What?'

'Hey! Hands off!'

I hung on all the harder.

'What did you say the name was?'

'Let go! Captivity hasn't improved your manners!'

I let go.

'La Sade,' she said, smoothing down her blouse. 'The Society for the Administration and Distribution of something or other.'

'Water,' I said. 'Is it a long way from the Colomers' house?'

'Just farther along the rue de la Gare.'

'Number 120?'

'What's special about 120? Is it a girls' boarding school? No, I don't know what number it is.'

'But is the rue de la Gare long enough to have a number 120?'

'I think so.'

'So let's get out of here,' I said to Faroux, 'and go and

find out why this mysterious number 120 rue de la Gare is so dangerous.'

'And don't come back without an apology,' said my ex-secretary.

Faroux answered for me.

'Inspector Faroux, Criminal Investigation Department,' he said, showing his card. 'I don't have as much reason as Monsieur Burma here to believe what you say. I'd appreciate it if you wouldn't leave here until further notice. And I warn you that if you do go anywhere you'll be followed.'

6 Another lonely house

'It's all becoming clear,' I said when we were sitting in the police Renault again. 'Once he had the cryptogram, Colomer went to the library and looked through the works of the Marquis de Sade. That gave him the number 120. The same day he got a card from his parents, telling him his father had got a job with La Sade. I didn't make the connection before because it was wrongly spelt. But that gave him the name of the street. He knows the district – he was born there.'

'How did he manage to locate the house so precisely?' Faroux growled. He'd been listening to me and giving orders to the driver at the same time.

'Because of the "Lion". He spelt it wrong when he copied the message down. Heredity. It should have been "from Lion", not "from Lyon". "Coming from Lion" refers to the Belfort Lion, the famous statue in the middle of the square at Denfert-Rochereau. And "after meeting the divine Marquis . . . the most prodigious . . . etc.," gives Sade and 120. The house we're going to is beyond the water company as you come from the centre of Paris. Let's hope we find out as much there as I did at Château-du-Loir yesterday. There are still plenty of points to clear up. How did Colomer get hold of the cryptogram in the first place? Why did he copy it down? How did he know the address was so important? And how did he link it all to Eiffel Tower Joe? We don't know the answers to any of those questions.'

'No,' said Faroux. 'Not to mention those about Georges Parris. What was he doing in uniform? Why did his torturers spare his life after all they'd put him through? Obviously not because they were squeamish.'

'Oh, I think I can explain that. The fighting was hotting up – no joke intended – in the area. They might be surrounded and have to move at any moment, and they didn't fancy leaving the body of a civilian behind where anyone might find it. They must have realized Parris's mind had gone and they wouldn't get anything out of him. So they untied him and stuck an old army uniform on him, then took him into the woods and shot him in the face. But they must have been jumpy, because the wound wasn't fatal and they ran away without making sure he was dead.'

'What an imagination! You tell it as if you'd been there.'

'Steady on! Don't reach for the bracelets yet. You're forgetting that Dynamite Burma's got what the Berniers and Farouxs of this world haven't got!'

The blackout was total, but I guessed we were going past the Belfort Lion by now, and gave it an ironical salute. We bowled down the avenue d'Orléans, and when we got to Alésia the driver stopped to consult a map.

'Avenue de Châtillon,' said the Inspector. 'Then the Rambouillet road as far as Maison-Blanche. Then turn left, and the first on the right is the rue de la Gare.'

'My God!' I exclaimed. 'To think we're so near, and the first time I heard it mentioned I was somewhere between Hamburg and Bremen.'

As we left Paris by the Porte de Châtillon we noticed searchlights probing the dark sky. We went on for fifty yards and the sirens began to wail. An alert.

'What's going on?' Faroux said in surprise. 'A test?'

'No,' I said. 'They're signing the Peace Treaty. Can't you hear the fireworks?'

Until now the sound of our engine had masked a distant anti-aircraft gun. But now a heavier battery opened up. Boom! Boom! A shell burst among the clouds with a dull thud.

'If we get there before the all clear,' I said, 'we'll probably catch the inmates down in the cellar.'

'What are we going to say to them?'

'Let's wait for the inspiration of the moment. But in any case we'll examine the building thoroughly. Hope it isn't a skyscraper.'

When we got to Maison-Blanche – which was pitch black – the guns were still going. Every so often the ground shook; the sky was bristling with searchlights. Then we went under a bridge and were at last in the rue de la Gare. It was covered in slush.

I told the driver to pull up beside a fence. Behind it rose a large white hoarding. The beam of my electric torch picked out the letters 'S.A.D.E.'.

'Go on,' I said. 'It can't be much further.'

The houses on either side were now very few and far between. For yards at a time we seemed to drive past nothing but waste ground. After frequent stops to peer at the numbers of the slumbering villas, we came at last to number 120.

The house stood at least a hundred yards from its nearest neighbour, and was surrounded by an iron fence set in a low wall. The lower of its two floors was built above ground level. The whole place was dismal and dark. When Faroux ordered the driver to turn his dimmed headlights on the façade, we could see that all the shutters were forbiddingly closed, except for one on the left which drooped from one hinge. I was filled with the same oppressive sadness as I'd felt the day before, looking at the house in the wood.

I noticed a bell on the gate and rang it. A jangling sound came from inside the house and died away in an echo. No sign of life followed. I rang again. Again no result.

'Strange. Because someone went in there not long ago – the snow's been trampled,' I said, shining my torch on the path leading from the gate to the steps up to the door.

'Look!' exclaimed the driver. 'There's a light upstairs!'

I looked up and swore.

'Call that a light?' I cried. 'Quick, Faroux – it's a fire!'

We hurled ourselves at the gate, but to the Inspector's surprise it opened easily. The front door was just as easy: it had already been forced, and what was left of the lock was hanging by one screw.

Inside, we quickly got our bearings and charged upstairs. We found ourselves in a large room. Tongues of flame were licking along one of the curtains, giving off a reddish glow. I ran forward past various objects which were strewn all over the floor, and it didn't take me long to put the fire out. We'd made it just in time.

There was the click of a light switch.

'The electricity's not working, sir,' said the driver. 'Unless there aren't any bulbs.'

I only had to play my torch across the ceiling to see it wasn't that.

'Go and look for the fuse box, Antoine,' said Faroux.

'And get out your revolver,' I added. 'There may be a prowler in the house. Whoever turned all this upside-down.'

'Right,' said the man. 'But I've left my torch in the car. May I borrow yours, Inspector?'

He moved towards Faroux.

'What's that noise?' I said.

'Me, sir,' Antoine answered. 'I trod on something. It felt like something small and round. It shot off somewhere.'

149

I shone my torch on the floor, but couldn't see anything amongst all the mess.

'We must have some more light,' I said. 'These torches are no good.'

'Go and find that fusebox,' Faroux repeated.

The driver went off and we waited, straining our ears for any suspicious sound. But there was only the scuffing of his shoes on the worn stair-carpet, the distant rumble of anti-aircraft guns, and the occasional whistle of a train from the nearby railway. Antoine came back. He hadn't found the fusebox, but he'd fetched a powerful spotlight from the boot of the car. So we could now examine the place properly.

A kind of chest of drawers had been dragged away from the wall, its marble top ripped off and its contents ransacked. All that was left of the etchings on the walls were the nails: the pictures themselves had been thrown in a corner, their frames torn away and the glass shattered. Some books lay scattered on the floor.

'Looks as if there's been a hurricane,' said the Inspector.

'Come, come,' I replied, 'I'm sure you've done just as well yourself in your time. Anyway, if it was a hurricane it was the kind of hurricane that smokes. That's how the fire must have started. A cigarette end, a scrap of paper, then the curtain. But it would have taken some time to catch properly – the visitor must have gone by the time we arrived. I was being over-cautious just now. We can put our guns away.'

'I saw the downstairs rooms while I was looking for the fusebox,' said Antoine in a noticeably louder voice. 'They're in the same shambles.'

'That doesn't surprise me. Someone's been making a systematic search.'

Sifting through the débris I discovered a hammer, the business end of which bore traces of white powder. And later, when we were examining the walls, we noticed hammer marks which could only have come from someone searching for a hollow place. Some plaster had come through a tear in the wallpaper. Faroux told us not to handle the hammer any further in case there were finger-prints on it. I doubted it.

In the end I found the cylindrical object the driver had trodden on. It was the shell-case from a Browning pistol. We soon found two more, but they seemed to be of a different calibre. As Faroux slipped them into his pocket my attention was caught by a heavy-looking curtain of dark red velvet which seemed to conceal an alcove. I decided to have a look, and edged round a chair to get nearer. To my amazement I saw a shoe, a woman's high-heeled shoe, protruding from the velvet folds.

I ripped the curtain back along its rod. There in the narrow space lay a girl, a torch beside her and one blood-stained hand clutching her breast. Her eyes were closed. The torch was out. She was wearing a well-cut suit and a beige raincoat. Her headscarf had slipped, freeing a mass of dark brown hair. It was the girl I'd seen in Perrache station. The mysterious girl in the trenchcoat whose photo-graph I'd found in Georges Parris's house. Her face was terribly pale. She seemed to be dead.

'She's alive,' said Faroux, straightening up. 'The pulse is weak, but she's alive. We'd better get her to hospital.'

'Very clever,' I said. 'You may be a policeman, but we'll still have problems doing that. Better take her to a doctor we can ask to keep his mouth shut. Someone who'll let us question her before she's completely recovered.'

'And I suppose you've got someone like that right up your sleeve?' he said.

'Exactly.'

I flicked through my notebook for Dorcières's address.

'Villa Brune. It's just round the corner – at the end of the rue des Plantes.'

'All right, we'll take her there. Any clues in the handbag, Antoine?' said Faroux.

'Her name's Hélène Parmentier,' answered the driver. 'A student.'

The Inspector didn't seem very impressed by that occupation.

'We can deal with all that later,' I said acidly. 'What we have to do now is—'

'Interesting though,' Faroux mused.

'I'd gladly exchange everything in the bag for a quarter of an hour's chat with its owner. If we hang around any longer we'll be taking her to the morgue, not the doctor's. Let's get moving. And the minute she opens her eyes I'm going to use all my charm to make her talk.'

He muttered something sceptical about Don Juan.

Antoine lit the way as we carried our attractive burden downstairs. She was still unconscious, but we made her as comfortable as we could in the back of the car. Faroux left the driver to keep watch in the house and took the wheel hmself. As we started up, the sirens started to wail again. The air-raid was over.

As we drove along I felt something hard against my hip and felt in the wounded girl's coat-pocket. An automatic pistol. I took it out and sniffed the barrel. It hadn't been used recently. It was the one I'd seen in her hand at the Perrache station. But I'd known for a long time that she hadn't fired then, either. I slipped the gun into my pocket. We'd arrived at the Villa Brune.

My ex-co-prisoner obviously did himself proud. It was a large and elegant house. The manservant who opened the door wasn't sure his master was in.

'Tell him his old friend Burma from the Stalag wants to see him urgently,' I said impatiently.

'And that Inspector Faroux is with him,' added Florimond.

The flunkey slithered off and vanished through a door off the hall, but he was soon back again. He couldn't look us straight in the eye. No, his master definitely wasn't in.

I elbowed him aside and with Faroux at my heels made for the door the servant had just closed behind him.

As we burst into the room a man in an expensive dressing-gown ran to a desk and pulled open a drawer.

'Another farcical entrance,' I said, rushing forward. 'Look out, Faroux, or he'll singe your moustache.'

I brought the edge of my hand down on Dorcières's wrist and his revolver dropped to the carpet. I kicked it out of reach.

'I hope you've got a permit,' I said. 'This man's a cop.'

'What does this mean?' Dorcières demanded.

'Just a little misunderstanding. I'm sure you'll be able to clear it up. But let's leave that for now. There's a seriously wounded patient waiting for you outside. We only came here to leave her in your care.'

Hubert Dorcières ran his hand over his eyes as if awakening out of a dream. His mouth twitched.

'Forgive me, Burma. I didn't recognize you, crashing in like that. But I'm sorry I went to pieces . . . Been overdoing it rather, lately . . . Your name had slipped my memory. I thought you must be a couple of impostors. So many of them about. There was a case in the papers only this morning . . . And as I've got a bit put away, I'm always terrified I'll be their next victim.'

He turned his blue eyes towards Faroux. The twitch had gone.

'Of course you don't believe me, Inspector.'

'Well . . . ' growled Faroux.

He'd grabbed the gun and was looking at it suspiciously. 'Have you got a permit?'

'Of course.'

He was about to go and look for it when I interrupted.

'The paperwork can wait. I can guarantee the doctor's respectability, Faroux. That should be enough. Let's get on with more serious matters.'

I told the doctor what we wanted him to do. Time was getting short.

'After what's happened I'm afraid I shan't be able to operate myself,' he said apologetically. 'My hands wouldn't be steady enough. But we can certainly take the patient to my clinic. My assistants are just as capable as I am. More so, in fact.'

He took off his dressing-gown, and the manservant, all agog, was sent to fetch a jacket and a fur-collared overcoat.

Five minutes later we were at the clinic. The surgeons on duty worked fast. The girl had a bullet lodged near her heart, and it had to be removed. But they couldn't guarantee success.

While they operated, Faroux and I sat in a chilly white waiting-room. Dr. Dorcières had some coffee sent in.

'Who is this quack?' said Faroux. He was sounding more and more suspicious. 'Do you believe his story?'

'Yes. His explanation of the way he behaved is quite plausible. And you can always make inquiries about him in the morning.'

'I might do that.'

'Then you must have plenty of energy to waste. As I haven't, I'm going to have a look at the girl's handbag. We can take our time about it now.'

We were in for some surprises.

7 Hélène

The papers in her bag showed the injured girl to be Hélène Parmentier, born on 18 June 1921. She had been living in Lyon, at 44 rue Harfaux, but according to a little card her present address was a hotel in the rue Delambre in Paris.

Looking through her other papers we were on familiar ground at once. There were three interesting photographs. The first was a group picture which included Robert Colomer. The second was of the prisoner who'd lost his memory. He looked in better shape then – shaved, with glasses and without the scar. The last was of Georges Parris before his transformation.

Faroux was crimson with excitement. Ferreting through the rest of the papers, he passed me a telegram. It was addressed to Mlle Parmentier, c/o M. and Mme Froment somewhere in Cap d'Antibes. It had been sent from Lyon the day I got back to France. The day of Colomer's death. It read:

'Don't bother leaving the station this evening. Wait for me on platform at Perrache. Surprise for you. Love and kisses. Bob.'

That wasn't bad. But the letter he gave me next was better. It threw a blinding and unexpected light on the girl's real identity. There was no date. This is what it said:

'My child,
When you receive this letter I shall no longer be in the land of the living. I know you won't reproach me for breaking the news to you so abruptly. We haven't been much like father and daughter to one another over the last few years. Ever since you found out my "profession" . . . Every time I write to you I inform a very reliable friend. He is to send the present letter on to you if ever he doesn't hear from me for six months. It's a kind of will. You'll find all you need to live comfortably for the rest of your life in a house you've never been to. But you know where it is and you have the keys. You know the place I'm talking about: *Coming from the Lion, after meeting the divine and infernal Marquis, this is the most prodigious of all his works.* (My love of word-games survives beyond the grave!) . . . '

'Your typical crook's mistrust, you mean!' said I.
 The letter went on:

'With most sincere affection' –

followed by an ornate signature in which the G and P were just discernible.
 A postscript followed:

'Ironic as it may seem . . . '

I turned the page:

' . . . it gives me pleasure to think that when you receive this letter it will be a kind of order of release. From now on you need never fear that harm can come to you through

Your loving father.'

Faroux tugged at his moustache.
 'She's Eiffel Tower Joe's daughter,' he said.
 'Looks like it. The famous Hélène he mentioned just before he died.'
 'That puts your secretary in the clear.'
 'Yes. I'll have to prepare some good excuses.'

'You'll manage. You always fall on your feet. So – what was the surprise Colomer had for the other girl? His own violent death?'

'I don't think so. But we can ask her about it soon. Just pass me the envelope this was in.'

It was square, yellow, and cheap. The address wasn't in the same writing nor in the same ink as the gangster's 'will'. I took the letter, examined it back and front with my magnifying glass, then folded it up and put it back in the envelope.

'The killer's cross-eyed,' said Faroux with a twinkle.

'No, left-handed,' I answered. 'But don't you notice anything strange?'

'About what?'

'The letter – the way it's folded. It's a normal sheet, but instead of being folded in four, as you'd expect, to fit the envelope, it's been folded in three and then in half again, which makes it too small for that size envelope.'

'Don't start talking in riddles like Georges Parris. I haven't got time to play games. Spit it out.'

'Originally the letter was in a long envelope sealed with red wax. And there was a small hole in the first envelope, which let a trace of the wax through. See this stain? You can have it analysed by anyone you like – I'll stake my life that it's wax. I reckon the "very reliable friend" Parris refers to wasn't as reliable as all that. He finds himself with a sealed letter he knows to be important – Parris hasn't made any secret of that. So he doesn't wait six months. He breaks the seal, reads the will and decides to grab the loot for himself. It must add up to a fortune, considering Joe's record. Of course he doesn't waste time trying to solve the riddle. It's practically indecipherable to anyone not in the know. Bob only managed it because of an extraordinary series of coincidences. The reliable friend goes straight to Parris and asks him nicely, in a romantic firelit setting, to spill the beans. You know what happens next. So the reliable friend goes home empty handed. He lets the six months elapse, by which time he can't use the old envelope – it's either been destroyed or is in too bad a state. So he takes the first one he can lay his hands on and sends the will to Hélène Parmentier.'

'So it's someone who knows her address and her real name.'

'What do you think! So he sends her the will, intending to follow her movements – he knows she'll lead him to the nest-egg sooner or later.'

'And it looks as if that's what happened. And he rewarded her by putting a hole in her. But how do you explain the fact that Colomer was able to copy the riddle down?'

'We can rule out the theory that Joe's daughter asked him to investigate.'

'Yes. She didn't need any help. From her father's letter it seems she knew what he was talking about. He didn't need to spell it out for her.'

Faroux paused, then said:

'The letter tells which house the treasure's in. But it doesn't say anything about *whereabouts* in the house it is.'

I didn't answer. I examined the letter again and noticed two pinpricks in the top left-hand corner.

'There's an extra sheet missing,' I said. 'A sketch or something like that, perhaps.'

'If so, the reliable friend's job would have been a lot easier—'

'But he never saw it. The PS wasn't written at the same time as the main text. Parris must have decided his letter was too cold and tried to soften it by adding something affectionate at the end. The paper that was pinned on the front was in the way, so he took it off . . . And then he forgot to put it back.'

'That's just supposition.'

'Corroborated by the facts. If the bloke had had the diagram, or whatever, do you think he'd have wrecked the whole house out at Châtillon?'

'No. Obviously not. I was going to make the same point myself five minutes ago.'

'So . . . You see?'

'Well, since you're so clairvoyant, tell me how Colomer managed to get his famous copy of the riddle.'

I put the letter down and turned to the envelope. After a moment I chuckled.

'What would you say if I proved that this "secret" message was read by quite a number of people? The second envelope was tampered with, just like the first! It was prised open. You can see that, even though the flap was very carefully stuck back. It was that old devil Bob the second time, I'm sure.'

'Intercepting other people's correspondence!' Faroux growled. 'Well, it didn't bring him any luck, did it?'

'Any more than it'll help the "reliable friend".'

'He's still on the loose,' sighed the Inspector. 'And he's probably got the loot.'

There was a knock at the door, and Hubert Dorcières came in.

'The operation's gone well,' he announced. 'The girl will be all right.'

'May we ask her some questions?' I said.

'Not yet. All in good time.'

'Look – don't forget you nearly welcomed a copper by blowing his whiskers off!' I said. 'We might be able to forget that incident if we can talk to the girl.'

Dorcières gave in.

'As you wish,' he said. 'But not yet. Let her have a few hours' rest.'

I turned to Florimond.

'That all right?'

'Yes. I've got several odds and ends to deal with. I'm going to requisition your telephone – er – doctor.'

Good old Florimond Faroux! Suspicious as ever. He even doubted the man's professional status.

'It's at your disposal,' said Dorcières. He moved towards the door, then stopped.

'Oh, Inspector,' he said. 'Here's the bullet we removed.'

Faroux took it and put it in his pocket. Then he went off to telephone. He gave orders for Antoine to be relieved of sentry duty in the rue de la Gare, and for Hélène Parris's room in the rue Delambre to be thoroughly searched.

'I've still got time to go to the office,' he said as he hung up.

'Good heavens. What for?'

'To pick up some information. About this doctor, and about the house in the rue de la Gare. It could wait, but I might as well take advantage of the few hours before we can speak to Mlle Parris.'

'Want me to come with you?'

'No. I'd prefer not to leave this fellow on his own. Keep an eye on him for me.'

I began to laugh.

'All right,' I said. 'We can exchange reminiscences.'

'Oh, you and your Stalag. No one will ever be allowed to forget you were a POW.'

'My dear Dorcières,' I said a few minutes later, pouring myself a fifth cup of high-grade coffee substitute, 'we seem destined to meet in unusual circumstances. First your sister was the victim of a blackmail plot, then we're both in the same prisoner-of-war camp, and tonight I bring you Miss Hélène Parris's charming body to hack about, and you nearly blow us to pieces.'

'I do beg you to forgive me,' Dorcières began, with a shudder.

'There, there. Let's say no more about it,' I said kindly. 'I've given Inspector Faroux my word the yarn you spun us was true. There's no more to be said.'

'Yarn! You mean—'

'That you're a liar. Yes. But there's no need to hold back now. There's only the two of us. You can settle down and tell me what really happened.'

'I've nothing to say,' he replied shortly. 'Your imagination's running away with you.'

'Really. Yet when I mentioned the injured girl's name – Hélène Parris, daughter of Eiffel Tower Joe – you started.'

'You're not infallible, M. Burma,' he replied. 'I assure you you're mistaken.'

'Well, let's say no more about that either,' I answered. 'All the same, I hope your local reputation bears examination. Inspector Faroux's gone off to inquire about it.'

'The Inspector will be wasting his time.'

'I'm sure he will,' I said. 'Just one last question. Did you go out yesterday evening?'

'I really don't see why I should answer. But no, I didn't.'

After this skirmish the conversation turned to trivial matters and remained there until the Inspector got back. He seemed agitated, and the doctor frowned. But Faroux spoke to him quite pleasantly, and as Faroux is the world's worst actor I concluded the reports he'd received were favourable.

'Can we see the girl now?' he asked.

'I'll go and find out,' said Dorcières, and left the room.

'Well,' I said, 'aren't you going to arrest him?'

Faroux shrugged.

'He's a model of virtue. Completely above suspicion. You were right. He just behaved like an idiot. But there's something else, something they told me happened at Montrouge. A car without lights ran a man over at Maison-

Blanche during the air raid. When they found him soon afterwards, he was dead. The wheels had gone right over him – that could be what killed him. But he also had two bullets in his stomach. Now Maison-Blanche isn't far from the rue de la Gare. I went to the Cochin Hospital to have a look at the body. His name was Gustave Bonnet. From Lyon. Funny that, don't you think? I didn't recognize him. Er – would *you* mind? Perhaps it would be better if *you* . . . '

'Sure it's not just so that you can question the girl on your own?'

Faroux protested indignantly.

'All right. I'll go. Write me a permit so I can use your car without any trouble.'

When I got back from Cochin I found Faroux chatting with Dorcières. They seemed quite friendly.

'Well?' said Faroux sharply, not giving me time to take my hat off.

'I had a look at the body. Not a pretty sight.'

'Seen him before?'

'No,' I said.

I was lying.

8 Disappearance of a flunkey

Hélène Parris lay in a spick and span bedroom with her dark brown hair tucked up under a little cap. She was whiter than the bedclothes and her breath came feebly.

When my hand touched hers she slowly opened her lovely wistful eyes and looked at me in astonishment.

'Good evening, mademoiselle,' I said, using the gentlest voice in my repertoire. 'I'm afraid we have to ask you some questions. We can't put it off any longer if we're going to avenge you and Bob. You knew him, didn't you? And I'd be surprised if he never mentioned me. I'm his boss. Nestor Burma.'

She closed her eyes in assent.

'You were at the station,' she said softly.

'Yes. And so were you. Why did you draw your revolver?'

'What's all this?' said Faroux angrily. 'You didn't tell me—'

'Bottle it, Florimond. The girl can't talk for long. Why *did* you have your gun out?'

'It was a reflex. I was waiting for Bob. He knew I was arriving that night and sent me a telegram telling me to wait on the platform. He said he had a surprise for me. I heard someone shout his name. It was you. He rushed towards you and . . . Oh, my God! . . . '

Dorcières leapt forward, his hands shaking and his nostrils flaring.

'She's in no fit state to be interrogated!' he said, bending over his patient, his tone unexpectedly firm.

I was perfectly well aware of that, but I had two more questions to put. The rest could wait.

'Just a little while longer, Mlle Parris. First, you don't deny that you're Hélène Parris, Georges Parris's daughter?'

'No.'

'Good – you're not responsible for your father's criminal activities. Now listen carefully and answer just as frankly. Did you see the man who shot Bob?'

'Yes.'

'And was he the man who went to the rue de la Gare last night?'

'Yes.'

'Did you know him?'

'Yes.'

'The name!' bellowed Florimond, rushing at the girl as though he was going to swallow her.

'Please! Be careful!' warned the doctor, seizing him by the arm. But the advice came too late.

'His name is . . . ' Hélène murmured. And lost consciousness again.

'Nothing more we can do for the moment,' I said. 'Better go and get some sleep. Anyway, I've found out all I wanted to know.'

The Inspector gave me a wry look.

'You're easily pleased,' he said.

A few hours later, and after much reflection, I'd just dropped off when I was awakened by the telephone.

'Hallo! Monsieur Burma?' came a lilting voice.

'Speaking.'

'Julien Montbrison here.'

'What a pleasant surprise! Are you in Paris?'

'Just for a few days. I finally got my wretched pass. Can we meet?'

'That depends. I'm pretty busy.'

'Hell!' he said, disappointed. 'I wanted you to do something for me.'

'What?'

'It's my valet. He insisted on coming to Paris with me, and he's disappeared.'

'And you want me to find him?'

'Yes.'

'I shouldn't worry about a little thing like that. He's probably with some blonde – and how do you think they'd like being disturbed?'

'Look, I'm not in the mood for jokes. He's a good fellow and—'

'Right. The phone always gives me a sore ear. Come and explain it all here over a drink.'

While I was waiting for him I called Faroux and asked if I could have another look at the house at Châtillon. He said I could.

'We've searched the flat in the rue Delambre,' he said. 'We found letters and cards confirming the girl is who she says she is. All sent from La Ferté-Combettes or Château-du-Loir, and signed G. Péquet.'

'Good. She must have used a false name to avoid awkward associations. Nothing more sinister than that, in case you were wondering. Any other news?'

'There's one other strange thing. But that goes without saying when you're involved. Ever since the 14th of this month, the girl's spent all her nights out and slept during the day. What do you make of that?'

'Ask her. When are you going to question her again?'

'Soon.'

'May I come? Don't bother to think before you answer. I'll be there anyway.'

He sighed and hung up.

I just had time to take a bath before Montbrison arrived to explain what was troubling him.

'He's a treasure, my valet. You must have seen him when you came to my house in Lyon. I'd be heart-broken if he'd met with an accident.'

'That's a big word. You've got good reason for using it, I suppose?'

'Yes. When he found out I was coming to Paris he asked if he could come with me. He even got a pass without saying anything about it. He produced it just as I was leaving, so though I was rather surprised I said he could come. No real reason why not. I like to be comfortable even when I'm travelling. Especially when I'm travelling.'

I said it was quite understandable.

'Yesterday I came across him by chance in a café. He was with a very suspicious-looking man. I heard them talking about someone called Joe or Jo – I couldn't make out if it was a man or a woman. When they saw me they separated, arranging to meet that evening at the Porte d'Orléans. And since then I haven't heard a word from Gustave. He's a good fellow, but not very bright. I'm afraid he may have got mixed up in some shady goings on.'

'Can you describe the other man and give me the name of the café? And would you recognize the chap if you saw him again?'

He said he would, and supplied the other information. I promised to look into the matter, but said it would be best to tell the police. He said he already had, but he didn't want to leave any stone unturned, and he had more confidence in me. I didn't argue.

'But even if the worst comes to the worst,' I said, 'you won't go into mourning for your valet. I'm having a little celebration here tonight. A war-time Christmas party. There'll be plenty of pretty girls. Starlets, in fact. Can I count on you?'

'And how! Starlets, eh?'

The portly lawyer took his leave. Too late I realized he'd told me nothing about his servant but his Christian name.

I made a series of phone calls inviting people to my Christmas get-together, and then went out. Walking along the boulevards, whom should I come across but Commissaire Bernier, listening to the patter of some hawker.

Marc, Montbrison and now Bernier. The whole of Lyon seemed to be in Paris. I brought my hand down on his shoulder.

'Papers!' I said.

The result was hilarious. First he went pale; then the veins on his nose went purple; finally he recognized me.

'You will have your little joke!' he said, shaking hands. 'How are you settling down in civvy street?'

'Loving every minute. And what brings you to these parts?'

'The Christmas holidays.'

'Are you free this evening? I'm having a little do at my place.'

I gave him the address.

'Do me the honour. Any time after eleven.'

'Good,' he said. 'We can have a little game of poker.'

We chatted for a while at the counter of a nearby café. Apparently all attempts to find Villebrun had failed. Bernier didn't once mention the fact a light had been seen in Jalome's flat at two o'clock in the morning. He was a typical civil servant. Always satisfied with the line of least resistance. As far as he was concerned, the policeman who saw the light had made a mistake and Jalome was obviously the killer. I had no reason to disillusion him. Yet.

I left him and made my way to Châtillon. The house was

no more attractive by daylight than it had been in the dark. The policeman on duty was flailing his arms like a windmill to keep himself warm. He'd been warned I was coming and let me poke about as much as I liked.

My next stop was Dorcières's clinic. He was there, looking drawn and tired. But when he spoke he was extremely firm.

'You can do what you like, but I will not be an accessory to murder. Tell everyone I drew a revolver on you. Put the worst possible construction on it – I don't give a damn. But I won't allow you to see my patient. Your last conversation, short as it was, left her terribly weak. You'll have to wait a few more days before you can talk to her again.'

'All right. Don't get excited. I hope it's nothing against me personally? I mean the same applies to Faroux, doesn't it?'

'Of course. I wouldn't let anyone . . . Not for anything in the world. I must and shall save that girl!'

He seemed strangely exalted. Professional conscience was all very well, but it seemed to me there must be more to it than that.

'Right,' I said. 'Faroux's on his way here, so I'll wait for him. Then I can be sure you're as strict with him as you are with me. Would you mind giving me a few sheets of paper? I always write a chapter of my memoirs when I have some time to spare.'

I didn't write my memoirs. I wrote this:

'Colomer meets H. P. and their friendship ripens into something more (see signature on telegram). Colomer suspects that Parris is alive and that H. is his daughter (establish when this suspicion began). To get more information he intercepts her mail. He sees that his suspicions are well founded and copies down the cryptogram. Why? The challenge. Because solving mysteries is his job. Becauses he wants to impress H. by decoding the mysterious document himself. (This would mean admitting he'd tampered with her correspondence, but Eros would see there was a happy ending). When he does finally solve the riddle, he's already returned the letter to H.'s flat (which explains why we find it on her). He intends to take H. to 120 rue de la Gare, but is shot at the station.

'Can we assume Colomer had noticed the letter wasn't in its original envelope? Yes. Because if he was shot down in Perrache station by the man who later searched number 120, that means Colomer must already have identified him and the other man knew it. But how did Colomer identify him? He knew he was an acquaintance of H.'s, the only one likely to be entrusted with the will. (If Colomer didn't know the man had tortured Parris, then he must have known something else, which I don't know but which put him on to his track.) We've already seen that this man, X, hadn't necessarily decided to kill Colomer. But when he saw Colomer run towards me he didn't hesitate. Conclusion: X knows me too.

'Why, once he's decoded the riddle, is Colomer in such a hurry to take H. P. to Paris that he sends her the telegram telling her to wait for him at the station, and decides to cross illegally into the occupied zone? Answer: he doesn't believe the man he suspects has solved the riddle, otherwise he wouldn't have sent the letter. The fact that he *has* sent the letter means he intends to follow the girl, assuming she has deciphered the cryptogram. So if H. leaves the station when her train arrives in Lyon she'll be in danger. In order to protect her, the best thing to do is tell her not to leave the station, and then persuade her to go straight on to Paris.'

I paused.

'Do you always stick your tongue out like that when you're writing to your sweetheart?' asked Faroux.

I put my jottings in my pocket and told him we weren't going to be allowed to see Hélène Parris. He was furious.

'But what more would you find out anyway?' I asked. 'And anyhow the dénouement's going to take place tonight in my flat. During my Christmas party, to which you're invited. And I'm going to give you a Christmas present: Colomer's killer, Parris's torturer and the man who wrecked 120 rue de la Gare.'

Faroux looked at me thoughtfully, twisting his moustache.

'That's a lot for one man,' he said.

But he seemed to think I might deliver the goods.

I got home just in time to pick up a call from Gérard Lafalaise.

'I haven't been letting the grass grow under my feet,' he said. 'Our friend was at Perrache station on the night of the murder. He managed to get through a police guard without much difficulty. He knew most of them, and it would never have occurred to them to suspect him. I think that's all now, don't you? My influential friends are beginning to wonder why I have to call the occupied zone so often.'

'Merry Christmas,' I said. 'And give Louise a kiss for me.'

9 The killer

It really was quite a party that gathered around my remaining bottles. Chubby Montbrison was there, rings flashing. And Marc Covet – I'd told him to bring his pen, and he'd have been the happiest man in the world if it hadn't been for his rheumatics. Simone Z. the starlet came, as pretty as a picture. And Louis Reboul, whom I introduced, truthfully, as one of the war's earliest casualties. Hélène Chatelain agreed to be present only after I'd gone down on my bended knees. A rubicund chap I introduced as Thomas, a painter, was really called Petit, and a cop, but it wasn't too obvious. Then there was Hubert Dorcières, with a face like a fiddle. I'd had to threaten him to make him come. He was the only one who didn't laugh at the jokes flying around, but his presence was essential: I was sure he'd be needed before the end of the evening. Finally there was an insignificant couple Marc had picked up at the 'Dôme', both of whom found my booze to their liking. And of course Faroux, who thanks to an ingenious system we'd set up for the purpose, was following everything that was said and done from an adjoining room.

After we'd listened to some music on the gramophone and played the truth game, in which everyone lies like a trooper, Simone put down her glass and said:

'Well, Burma, how about telling us one of your adventures? As a detective, I mean!'

The rest wouldn't take no for an answer, so I began.

'Once upon a time,' I said, 'a well-known gangster, in order to throw off his pursuers, arranged a fake death and then got a plastic surgeon to work on his face. And I must say he made a great success of the operation. A real masterpiece.'

I was the only person to notice that Dorcières went horribly pale and emptied his glass in one.

'This man had a daughter . . . '

And I went on to tell the story of the will, the 'friend's' betrayal of his trust, the 'heated' discussion between the two men, and so on.

'The torturers think they've killed him. But they haven't, and fate decrees that he's captured by the Germans, cured of his physical though not of his psychological wounds and sent off to a prisoner-of-war camp. Where who should be wasting his sweetness on the desert air but—'

'The inimitable Nestor Burma!' yelled Marc Covet.

'Exactly. Well, in the prison camp the man dies, this time for real, and more or less in my arms. With his last breath he whispers an address. End of act one.'

I handed my glass to Simone to refill. She drank it herself. The argument that ensued was interrupted by pleas for me to go on with the story. Though still without a drink, I did so.

I told of my dramatic encounter with Colomer and his death, when the mysterious address cropped up again like a sinister leitmotif.

'Now let's get back to the "reliable friend",' I said. 'He goes home empty handed and waits out the six months. Then he sends the will to the beneficiary through the post. Why through the post? He was certainly intended to deliver it in person. But he doesn't do so because of the missing envelope. This way, if the girl notices anything suspicious he can always deny ever having had the letter. It doesn't mention the name of the friend. Once he's sent it, all he has to do is follow her and she's sure to lead him to the loot. But now there's a slight hitch. The girl suddenly decides to go away, and she's already in the train by the time the postman drops the letter in her box. All our friend can do is wait for her to go home again. This is where Colomer comes in. He seems to have had a very special place in Mlle Parris's heart, and knows her movements. He has intercepted the famous letter, looking for proof that she's Eiffel Tower Joe's daughter. He realizes the letter's been opened, or rather that it's not in the original envelope. He notices, just as I did later, the strange way the letter's folded in relation to the size of the envelope, and the slight trace of wax on it. Moreover, he notes that the postmark is that of the post office nearest the house of Hélène Parmentier's "banker". That is, the man who acts as intermediary when her father wants to send her money. (This is an oversight that will have incalculable consequences for the torturer.) Colomer copies out the cryptogram and tries to decipher it. He succeeds on the very day the girl is coming back, and decides to return to Paris with her. But Colomer's future killer has got wind of his suspicions, thinks Bob knows more than he does, and decides to eliminate him. Maybe Bob is instinctively careful in the dark and empty streets. Anyhow, he prevents the killer from carrying out his plan up to the time when he goes to the Perrache station. Perhaps the killer himself is weighing up the pros and cons and isn't certain what to do – I don't know. But what I do know is that when he sees Colomer rush towards me he doesn't hesitate any longer. No point in being modest. When he sees me he panics! He's afraid Colomer's going to tell me everything. So he fires.

'Later he finds out from Carhaix, alias Jalome, that I'm

looking for a girl who's the spitting image of Michèle Hogan, the film star. He's so worried he makes the same mistake with me as he did with Bob. He overestimates how much I know, and arranges the attack on the Pont de la Boucle. He stays nearby to watch, and when he sees what happens makes a bee-line for Carhaix's flat to destroy anything that might establish a link between them. He knows the Lyon police think Colomer was killed for revenge. So he leaves the gun he murdered Bob with in the flat. He knows it's bound to incriminate Carhaix, especially as he's an ex-colleague of both Eiffel Tower Joe and Villebrun. So that's how X manages to hoodwink the police. And me too, apparently.

'It all seems sown up. Now that he knows where to find it, all our friend has to do is go and pick up the inheritance. I suppose he heard Bob call out the address just before he died. It was a revelation to X, who as Joe's factotum, "Monsieur Péquet", thought he knew all about him.

'So yesterday, our Monsieur X arrives in Paris, goes to the house, turns it upside down, but finds nothing. Then he goes back again during the night. Why? Because in the meantime he's had an idea. On his first visit he looked for complicated hiding places. But he suddenly remembers Edgar Allan Poe's famous story, *The Purloined Letter*, which suggests that the safest hiding place is the most obvious. He goes back to the abandoned house and puts his theory to the test. He has an accomplice, who certainly took part in the dramatic events at La Ferté-Combettes and who has so much confidence in his boss that he won't let him out of his sight. They find the loot, and the accomplice tries to shoot X but misses. The bullet goes through a curtain and seriously wounds someone hidden behind it. X then fires back and doesn't miss; we already know from Perrache that he's a very good shot. The accomplice has just enough strength to run away into the night. It's pitch dark because of the blackout. The snow has melted into slush and nothing shows up against it, so he manages to get away. But he soon collapses in the road, and is later run over by a car driving without lights.'

I stopped. They were hanging on every word.

'Moreover,' I went on, 'X, who has killed several times, is here tonight.' This produced what parliamentary reports call a 'sensation'.

'Yes,' I repeated, 'the killer is here. Which of you is it? It's someone who knows Colomer, and the beneficiary of the will, and yours truly. From certain observations I made at "The Retreat", he tends to be left-handed. While Joe was tied to the chair he was punched several times on the right cheek. At one point he must have moved his head to avoid one of the torturer's blows. It grazed the chair instead, on the left side as you look at it. What kind of people use their left hands? Left-handed people of course, but also those, for example, whose right arm has been amputated.'

All eyes turned to Louis Reboul.

He made a feeble attempt at a smile. Not a pretty sight.

'And what about the attack on the Pont de la Boucle?' I continued. 'Marc Covet didn't seem to be struggling very hard. Was he only pretending?'

'How dare you!' said Covet, leaping from the divan, scarlet with rage. 'Why, you lousy—!'

'Put a sock in it,' I said. 'Ladies present. Let's continue our inquiry.'

I turned to the girl from the 'Dôme'. 'Would you say M. Covet was left-handed, my dear, from your experience?'

'No,' she said, blushing.

But nobody felt like laughing.

An uncomfortable silence ensued.

Then several of the guests started. It was the front-door bell.

'Open the door, please,' I said to Reboul. 'And don't go running off.'

He came back with Commissaire Bernier. The clock struck eleven.

'On the dot,' I observed as Reboul took the policeman's coat and hat. 'My dear fellow, are you still convinced that Colomer's killer and the man who tried to chuck me in the Rhône are one and the same person? That is, Jalome, alias Carhaix, now deceased?'

'Of course,' he stammered. 'But what's going on here? You should see all your faces! Anyone would think you were at a wake!'

'We almost are.'

'I came to have a good time!'

'And so you shall. At the truth game. I'm about to introduce you to the killer. He's in excellent health; nothing ghost-like about *him*. You can shake him by either hand; he's ambidextrous. I told you all about a graze on the chair just now, didn't I? It's extremely important. When he was hitting Joe, the man damaged one of his rings and lost a stone out of it. Montbrison, would you mind showing me the rather vulgar signet ring you wear on the little finger of your left hand?'

'Not at all,' he said, coming forward with his usual ingratiating smile. 'Not at all.'

Screams from the ladies, oaths from the men and a general rush for shelter greeted the two shots that then rang out. Montbrison had fired through the left pocket of his jacket. I felt a searing pain in my right arm. One bullet had glanced off the bullet-proof vest I was wearing underneath my waistcoat. The second had made a hole in a Magritte that was hanging on the wall.

10 *The accomplice*

When the tumult had abated I saw that Hélène Chatelain was beside me. She'd been the first to rush forward to help. I could see she'd forgiven me for my unjust suspicions. A good girl, that.

'Didn't I warn you you'd be needed?' I said to Dorcières. 'Though you didn't seem bowled over by the idea.'

'Well, I—' he began. Then brusquely: 'Let's have a look at that arm.'

He said it was nothing serious.

Faroux had emerged from hiding and stood by the chair on which Montbrison now sat, the flashy rings on his fingers no brighter than the bracelets on his wrists. 'Thomas' had disappeared.

I held up the piece of 'glass' I'd dug out of the chair at 'The Retreat' and placed it beside the signet ring. It exactly matched the original stones and showed up the replacement for what it was.

'You shouldn't have used your gun just now,' I told him quietly.

'Foolish reflex,' he agreed good-humouredly. 'Mere exasperation. I thought I might as well take you with me. I might have known you'd taken precautions . . . Have you suspected me from the start?'

'No. I didn't begin to suspect you seriously until after

Jalome attacked me. When I went to his flat at three-thirty the next morning with Lafalaise and Covet—

'I'll explain all this later, Commissaire,' I said to Bernier, whose eyes were coming out on stalks.

'I hadn't smoked for some time – my pouch was empty, thank God, and I can't stand cigarettes. So when I went in, before the others, I noticed the smell of a particular kind of Virginia tobacco. I also noticed there were spent matches in the ashtray. Had Jalome been smoking before he left? No. The smell was too strong. Someone had to have smoked there more recently. And even if Jalome smoked (we did find a packet of Gauloises in his pocket later) he didn't use matches. There were none in the flat except in the ashtray. But there *were* several containers of lighter-fuel. So someone else had been in the flat. Who? Someone who smoked Virginia tobacco and was such a heavy smoker he couldn't stop even in circumstances like these. Where had I already come across that smell? In your house, Montbrison, and nowhere else. And then certain details and discrepancies came back to me which hadn't seemed important before. First, your statement to the Lyon police. The fact that you went to them twenty-four hours late. You spent the interval trying to decide whether or not you should admit to knowing Colomer, didn't you? But even more striking was the *attitude* you adopted in your statement. I mean the description you gave of poor old Bob. He hadn't seemed panic-stricken when I saw him at the station. Yet you described him to me as being absolutely overwrought. You talked of fear and anxiety, about his being the target of some revenge plot and I don't know what else. Not to mention the business about drugs. As if a habit like that doesn't show in someone's face. You don't have to be a doctor to know that. I was suspicious because you seemed so ignorant on that score. Yet you used the technical term "withdrawal symptoms", and when you described your eye complaint you used the rather esoteric expression, "amblyopia".'

'What's that when it's at home?' said Faroux.

'A condition produced by nicotine poisoning. A semi-paralysis of the optic nerve, leading to colour-blindness. Hence his witty answer to my question "Was Colomer in a blue funk?": "I couldn't say – I suffer from amblyopia." Not that that makes him smoke any less. Tobacco's more important to him than anything. *He*'s really the one who's a drug addict. The soft spot he's always had for alcohol is nothing in comparison. He keeps a whole stock of Philip Morris, but nothing whatever to drink. And the Philip Morris were his downfall.'

I turned to Montbrison.

'When I came to see you I said it was to ask your advice, but it was really to test my theory. And there it was again. That smell, coming from the cigarette you were smoking. And your ashtray was overflowing with the same kind of matches as I'd found at Jalome's. Either the manservant hadn't emptied it, or you'd already smoked enough to fill it again before I arrived. You were in a dressing-gown, but you still had your rings on, and your hands were cold and not as clean as they would have been if you'd just got up. I don't think you'd even been to bed. You were probably too anxious to know how things were going to turn out to be able to sleep.

'You must have been scared when you saw me turn up so early in the morning, and I can imagine your relief when I seemed not to be hostile. But while you were beginning to relax I was starting to sniff out a trail. And there were one or two other examples of unusual behaviour on your part – nothing that would convince a jury, but they helped me on my way. When we rolled out of the restaurant that evening, for instance, you kept on about putting me up for the night. I refused your invitation, but you insisted on walking me back to the hospital, cold as it was. You obviously had some ulterior motive. If Marc Covet hadn't tagged along I don't know if I'd still be here now playing Sherlock Holmes.'

'Your theory about matches, cigarette-ends, etc., doesn't really add up to much,' said Montbrison with a cynical laugh.

'In the usual course of events, no. But we live in unusual times. There isn't exactly a glut of Philip Morris, as I found out when I sounded out the black market. They offered me sugar, condensed milk, elephants and first editions. But no Philip Morris, not even when I offered a hundred francs a cigarette. You stocked up in time. Though I don't think they'll be much good to you now . . . So it was you in Jalome's flat when the policeman saw the light – you've got a servant to draw the curtains for you at home, so it didn't occur to you to bother about the black-out there. When the policeman rang to complain, you didn't answer. And I don't blame you.'

I took a sip of my drink, then said:

'Anyway, even before I noticed that Hélène Parris's letter had been franked at the post office near where you live, my trip to La Ferté-Combettes showed me I was definitely on the right track. I remembered having heard the name of the village before. Arthur Berger, the war correspondent, had mentioned it. You bumped into him on 21 June, the day you tortured Parris and left him for dead. The day Parris was taken prisoner, and you yourself were slightly wounded by a stray bullet. Then I found evidence that you'd been in the house – the brilliant caught in the chair. And also what old Monsieur Mathieu told me. He'll have no difficulty identifying you as "Monsieur Péquet". We're not short of witnesses. And I still haven't mentioned Hélène Parris, who was standing only a few yards away when you shot Bob.'

'God Almighty!' he spluttered.

'You thought she was miles away. No wonder you didn't notice her – you were completely absorbed in what you were doing. And the policemen searching for the killer afterwards left you alone: you knew a lot of them, as you said, and you were the last person they'd suspect. They were probably looking for someone with a five days' growth of beard and a knife between his teeth—'

I was interrupted by a strident blast from the telephone.

'Someone asking for Inspector Faroux,' said the person who picked it up.

'Hallo!' Florimond shouted. 'Is that you, Petit?'

He had a short conversation and hung up.

'Very interesting,' he said. 'I sent Petit to check up on the gun we just took off our friend here. The bullets are identical to the ones we found in Gustave Bonnet's body last night.'

'Oh, I was forgetting!' I exclaimed. 'Gustave Bonnet, the servant and second accomplice! Montbrison walked into the lion's den this morning and told me his valet had disappeared. An amusing yarn, but it didn't work. Actually you've been very sporting, Montbrison – coming to the party and all . . .'

'I didn't expect it to turn out so badly,' he said.

'Petit told me something else,' Faroux went on. 'Bonnet had a gun in his kit, too. He fired the shot that nearly killed Hélène Parris.'

I turned to Montbrison.

'And the loot,' I said evenly. 'Where is it?'

'I didn't find it,' he replied.

'Come, come. That's not nice,' I said reproachfully. 'Just when I've been saying how sporting you are. I'm afraid I'm going to have to have you searched.'

I gave Faroux a look. But Bernier got there first, and he didn't use kid gloves. However:

'Nothing,' he said when he'd finished.

'What about that?' I said, pointing with my good hand at a little bottle, one of the articles removed from the lawyer's pockets. It was almost hidden by a handkerchief and was half-full of rough-textured pills. It bore a red label, indicating that its contents were toxic.

'Good Lord,' exclaimed Bernier. 'There's enough here to poison a regiment!'

I laughed.

'Edgar Allan Poe!' I said. 'Amongst the ink-bottles and pots of glue on the mantelpiece in the house in the rue de la Gare I found the carton this bottle came in – it had been opened, but only recently, because there was no dust inside. Eiffel Tower Joe's savings are in that bottle.'

'Poison pills?'

'Oh, they're certainly lethal! But not via the digestive system.'

I asked my ex-secretary to open the bottle, and she tipped one pill into the palm of her hand. I told her to scrape the surface with a knife. Which she did, revealing a pearl: when all the plaster was removed we could see it was a natural orient pearl of the highest quality.

'There are fifty of these in the bottle,' I said. 'I don't know how many millions of francs they're worth!'

'Did you guess what the document was, attached to the will and mislaid by the person forwarding it?' Faroux asked.

'What I thought was a diagram or sketch? No. But now we can be pretty sure it was some sort of picture to guide Hélène Parris to the hiding place. A picture of a bottle, for example . . . Cut out of the same catalogue that my friend Bébert used, to make the cone for collecting his cigarette ends.'

A little later Montbrison, who seemed to have regained his poise, if he'd ever lost it, coolly told us how he'd met

Parris. Several years before, he'd worked for the lawyer defending the gangster, and Eiffel Tower Joe, who was a shrewd judge of character, realized Montbrison might be useful to him.

I'd known about this ever since my research in the National Library.

Montbrison then went on to tell about Jalome.

'He was with us at "The Retreat". He'd known Hélène for a long time. They used to go out together sometimes. He'd told her he'd given up crime and settled down. She's a respectable girl, even if she *is* a gangster's daughter.'

'That didn't stop her accepting money acquired dishonestly.'

Montbrison shrugged.

'She wasn't trained for anything. Everyone has to live. And she was working to get some qualifications so as to be independent . . . You said she was in the house at Châtillon . . . But if she was looking for her inheritance, she certainly didn't intend to keep it.'

There was a knock at the door. It was a driver from police HQ, come to pick up the package, as he put it.

Montbrison bowed ironically to everyone and started to leave, escorted by the policeman. The driver opened the door. Montbrison slipped and fell flat on the floor. Faroux thought it was some kind of escape attempt and threw himself on top of the lawyer, kicking a small round object towards me. It was what had caused the killer's fall. Intrigued, I picked it up. It was round and white like the contents of the bottle. I asked where the bottle was.

'In my pocket,' the Inspector replied.

'Take it out.'

Faroux obeyed. The top was still screwed on tight.

There was no time to see whether the theory germinating in my brain was correct or not. The door was open. I had to move fast. I took my revolver in my good hand and, risking my reputation and my freedom, pointed it at the group. In a trembling voice I said:

'Faroux, old chap – have you ever arrested one of your superiors before?'

'Bernier was a gambler,' I said a few hours later in front of a reduced but attentive audience. 'When we first met, in the hospital, he was in evening dress. He'd just come out of some gambling joint. When I got back to Paris, Faroux asked me if the Commissaire Bernier I was talking about was the same one he'd known years before. It was. He told me Bernier had been moved away from Paris because of some shady dealings. He'd only kept his post thanks to his political connections. When Montbrison, whom he'd met at his club, suggested he should lead the investigation off on the wrong track and get the case hushed up, he agreed. He needed the money for his gambling. So he accepted Montbrison's explanation blindly, and tried to make me do the same. He did all he could to make me believe in Jalome's guilt – he even let me go with him to the flat to witness the discovery of the revolver. He tried to incriminate Lafalaise, and disregarded the report about the light that had been seen in Jalome's flat. And as I didn't tell all I knew, he didn't realize I knew it. Nor did Montbrison. That's why they both agreed to come to the party. It is Christmas after all, and they made the mistake of thinking I'd come back from POW camp completely soft in the head.

'When Montbrison slipped on the pearl, I wondered where it had come from. Not from the bottle, because the top was still firmly screwed on. And why wasn't the bottle full? Was there another accomplice among us, with his part of the spoils still on him? Someone who'd carelessly let it fall from his pocket when he took his coat off? All my guests had taken their own coats off in the hall except Bernier. He'd taken his off in front of us, and Reboul had folded it over his arm and taken it outside to hang it up. It was then that a pearl from the other tube, which must have come undone, fell on to the hall carpet. Apart from my old friend Covet, Bernier was the only other person here who was from Lyon. (I know I got at Covet during the course of the evening, but that was only play-acting, designed to unnerve the really guilty person.) But Bernier had no real reason to be in Paris for the festivities. He has no family here, and his former colleagues in the police give him the cold shoulder. He rushed to search Montbrison, but tried to hide the bottle when he found it. I understood Montbrison's sardonic smile as he left us. The Colomer case would be heard in Lyon, and he was counting on Bernier to make it easy for him to escape. All this flashed through my mind in a second. I didn't think any more, I risked everything and acted.'

'And so,' said Hélène Chatelain, 'we found the other half of the swag on the pillar of the law.'

11 The first murder

Next day Hélène and I went to the clinic; we'd been told the other Hélène was a lot better. It was a fine day, and the snow sparkled in the sun. I thought of poor old Bob. He used to love winter sports.

'He was a good lad, old Colomer,' I said. 'There he was, mortally wounded – he didn't know by whom – and all he thought about was passing on to me what he'd found out about Georges Parris. He just said "120 rue de la Gare", and counted on my being ingenious enough to follow it up.'

'Yes,' said Hélène, 'the Fiat Lux Agency will certainly miss him.'

As soon as we arrived at the clinic Hubert Dorcières rushed to greet us, looking ten years younger.

'We've saved her!' he exclaimed. 'I'm so happy!'

He shook us both by the hand as though we'd performed the operation ourselves. Then he took us to Hélène's bedside.

'So you're going to be all right, are you?' I said. 'I'm delighted. Especially as I've still got a few questions to ask you. Mustn't neglect my job.'

'More questions!' she sighed. She had a sweet, musical voice that was very affecting.

'Just a few details.'

I asked my questions and she answered them. This is the substance of what she told us:

It had been a reflex that made her pull out her revolver when she saw Montbrison shoot Bob: an atavistic impulse, you might say. She'd been full of a whole complex of emotions, including the desire for revenge and the fear of becoming Montbrison's second target. But the safety catch of her pistol, which she carried only out of child-like bravado, had been on so long it was jammed, and you couldn't pull the trigger. She'd managed to leave the station by an exit the police hadn't yet closed off, and went straight home. There she'd found the will waiting for her, and linked it at once to the address Bob had shouted out just before he died. But she couldn't understand how he'd found it out. (Not wanting to sully her memory of him, I didn't enlighten her.) She took the first train across the border to the occupied zone, though she hadn't got a pass. Once in Paris she spent every night in the house at Châtillon, searching for the treasure. She didn't want to keep it, and intended to hand it over secretly to the police. The evening we found her wounded, she'd come to the house and found the door had been forced during the day. The whole place had been ransacked. Later she heard the visitors coming back, and hid in the alcove. She recognized Montbrison and his valet, and the rest had happened as I'd imagined.

I stroked her slim hand.

'That's one nightmare over,' I said. 'Did you ever tell Colomer who you really were?'

'No.'

'He suspected it though. Do you know how?'

'He probably noticed a photo of father I had in my flat. And one day I did a stupid thing.'

'What was that?'

'I was born on 10 October 1920, not 18 June 1921. Last year, for no particular reason as far as I know, Bob brought me some flowers on the tenth of October. When I thanked him I said it was very kind to bring me flowers on my birthday. I corrected myself straight away and invented some story. But he must have thought it was strange—'

'Probably. And as the fact that your father had a child, and its date of birth, were mentioned in some newspaper articles – not the cuttings he had: longer articles like the ones I read at the National Library – his suspicions were confirmed.'

We were silent a moment. Then I said:

'What will you do when you get out of here?'

'I don't know,' she replied. Her voice was tired and her magnificent eyes more moving than ever. 'I'm afraid your friend the Inspector will have some plans for me. I've been using false papers.'

'Tsk, tsk,' I said. 'He'll turn a blind eye to that. No one will bother you when you walk out of here. And if anything goes wrong, come and see me.'

'Thank you, Monsieur Burma,' she murmured. 'Bob often talked about you. He said you were a very good chap.'

'It depends on the day,' I said, smiling. 'But with you I'll always be just as nice as you like. Funny thing, fate. From now on, your father's old enemies will be your best friends.'

When we said goodbye those lovely wistful eyes were misty.

Dorcières insisted on escorting us to the front door, and then almost crushed our hands in his slim surgeon's fingers. There was no sign of the haughtiness I'd known in the prisoner-of-war camp. He was a different man.

'I'm so happy to have saved her,' he said. 'How can I ever thank you for bringing her to me?'

'Well!' Hélène chuckled as we went round the corner. 'Dorcières is in the seventh heaven. Is he in love or something?'

'No,' I said, grabbing her arm and stopping her dead. 'That's not it. By the way, this investigation's going to be good publicity for me. I think I'd like to reopen the agency. Are you ready to drop Readall's?'

'Am I!' she exclaimed, genuinely pleased.

'Then I can tell you everything and you'll understand why Dorcières is so happy to have saved the girl. How many murders do you think there have been?'

'Two. Bob Colomer and Gustave the valet . . . Oh, and Jalome. I think that's all.'

'You're forgetting the most important corpse. Georges Parris.'

'But he died of natural causes.'

'No. Dorcières gave him an injection.'

Hélène was so surprised she let out a little shriek.

'He was the plastic surgeon who worked on Parris,' I explained. 'He agreed to do it out of a mixture of pride and scientific curiosity. The operation was a brilliant success. But Parris wasn't any more to be trusted than his friend Montbrison. He showed his gratitude to Dorcières by going off with his mistress. (We don't know what happened to her.) Dorcières was outraged, but he couldn't get his revenge. If he denounced Joe he'd expose himself and lose both his job and his honour. For the same reasons he didn't want to set a trap and bump him off. But as I said a few minutes ago, fate is strange. Dorcières found himself face to face with him in the POW camp hospital. He had him completely at his mercy. The man was just a number, and his memory had gone. It was an opportunity he'd never dreamed of. But he had to be careful. There was a man in the camp he couldn't underestimate. And that man was . . .'

' . . . my subtle and intelligent boss,' chirped Hélène.

'In the bone rather than the flesh,' I said. 'But how much

did Burma know about the man who'd lost his memory?
The best way to find out was to have a talk with him.
That's why Dorcières came up to me all of a sudden, even
though he'd known who I was for a long time and never
bothered to renew our acquaintance. But our conversation
didn't enlighten him much, and when I asked him to find
me a job at the hospital the idea obviously didn't appeal to
him. He promised he would, but he did nothing about it.
Anyway, I got the job all the same. While I was there he
wouldn't try anything against Parris. It was the day I wasn't
there that he committed his . . . '

'Crime?'

'I hesitate to use the word, because Eiffel Tower Joe had
really asked for it. Anyhow when a person has lost his
memory . . . He did him a good turn, really.'

'You have such an original way of looking at things.'

'I'm certainly more cynical than the doctor. He's been
eaten up with remorse ever since. He went completely to
pieces and was capable of any rashness, as we saw the
other night. When the valet told him Burma and a police
inspector had come to see him, he thought I knew everything and that we'd come to arrest him.'

'So I suppose he was trying to atone for his crime by
saving his victim's daughter?'

'Yes. If he hadn't succeeded I think he'd have killed
himself. But now he's a different man. Excuse me a
moment . . . '

We were just passing a flower shop. When I came out
Hélène said:

'Are they for Mlle Parris?'

'Yes,' I replied.

She took my arm and looked me straight in the eye.
There was a mischievous glint in her own.

'Nestor Burma,' she said. 'Do you mean to tell me—?'

'Of course not,' I said, disengaging myself. 'What, a private detective and a gangster's daughter?'

'You'd make a fine pair,' she said. 'But what on earth would the children be like?'

Paris, Châtillon, 1942

All Pan books are available at your local bookshop or newsagent, or can be ordered direct from the publisher. Indicate the number of copies required and fill in the form below.

Send to: **CS Department, Pan Books Ltd., P.O. Box 40, Basingstoke, Hants.   RG21 2YT.**

or phone: 0256 469551 (Ansaphone), quoting title, author and Credit Card number.

Please enclose a remittance* to the value of the cover price plus: 60p for the first book plus 30p per copy for each additional book ordered to a maximum charge of £2.40 to cover postage and packing.

*Payment may be made in sterling by UK personal cheque, postal order, sterling draft or international money order, made payable to Pan Books Ltd.

Alternatively by Barclaycard/Access:

Card No. ☐☐☐☐☐☐☐☐☐☐☐☐☐☐

Signature:

Applicable only in the UK and Republic of Ireland.

While every effort is made to keep prices low, it is sometimes necessary to increase prices at short notice. Pan Books reserve the right to show on covers and charge new retail prices which may differ from those advertised in the text or elsewhere.

NAME AND ADDRESS IN BLOCK LETTERS PLEASE:

....

Name ——————————————————————————

Address ————————————————————————

————————————————————————————

————————————————————————————

————————————————————————————

3/87